A Packet of Seeds

Ian Nicholson

ISBN: 9798695293326

Cover illustration: Ian Nicholson

www.moderngothicwriter.com

This book is dedicated to Toni Mount, Sue Jeeves and Mike Swift for all their encouragement and for planting the initial seeds.

SEED CATALOGUE

BATH TIME

They will bob up and down displaying those ridiculous upturned beaks for months, even years in some cases, heading who knows where. Either someone had deliberately released them, or a container had overturned and spilled its contents into the sea, leaving the irritatingly cute little creatures to slowly spread across the oceans.

They will be washed ashore in many countries, including France, America, India and Spain, but our focus today is on Ninety Mile Beach in New Zealand. A six-year-old boy is running over the pale sand towards Sally, his mother, holding something bright yellow in his left hand. He passes it to her, and she reflects the beaming smile on its plastic face.

'Can I keep it, Mum? Please let me keep it!'

'Well I suppose so, Max. It's been washed clean by the sea so it can't do any harm. What do you think, Katie? Do you like it?'

Sally dries the toy with a stripy beach towel before passing it to Max's little sister. Katie is just four and loves playing on the beach, especially when there's a picnic involved. Because yellow is her favourite colour, the gaudy object easily meets with her approval. She throws it onto the sand and screams with delight, and Max rushes to grab what he already sees as his own personal treasure.

'It's mine! It's mine! She can't have it!'

'Don't be horrible to your sister, Max. You did find it, yes, but you need to learn to share your things more. If I let you keep it, you must agree to let Katie play with your little yellow mate, too. Bath times will be more fun for both of you now!'

Max scowls at his sibling, who claps her hands together with innocent glee. The late afternoon sun is losing its strength, so Sally announces that it's time for them to head home. She asks Max to help pack everything up, which he does with a shrug and a sigh, but makes sure he keeps hold of his new possession by stuffing it all the way down in his rucksack.

~~~~

Sally loads the dishwasher after an early tea then sits at the kitchen table, watching her youngsters playing on a large blue rug in the garden. She hates to admit it, but she misses Finn more than ever at times like these. Determined not to let memories of their acrimonious divorce sweep in and spoil such a lovely moment, Sally stands up and calls through the patio doors.

'Max! Katie! It's bath time!'

~~~~

The water gushes out of the mixer tap as Sally helps Katie to undress. Max is down to his boxers already, and suddenly realises he's forgotten something. He runs through to the bedroom and almost rips the zip off his rucksack, so eager is he to retrieve the duck. He goes back to the bathroom to find Katie giggling excitedly in a mass of bubbles.

'Climb in, Max. Oh, good! I see you've brought your new friend, but don't forget what I said about sharing.'

Max knows that his mother is right, but he doesn't respond. He slips off his shorts and gets into the bath, still tightly holding the smiling creature. Max slides into the suds with the duck held aloft.

Under Sally's instruction, he drops it into the soapy water and parts the bubbles so that Katie can see it, but then something strange happens. The plastic bird, until now merely solid and faintly comical, begins to shake and shudder.

'How odd, Max! It must be the hot water or the steam that's causing it. That's funny, isn't it, Katie?'

The little girl squeals with pleasure as the yellow thing jerks from side to side, becoming more animated by the second. Max just stares at it, but his mother is unnerved by the whole situation, which is exacerbated when the object mysteriously stops moving. The bathroom is completely silent, apart from the gentle fizzing sound of soap bubbles bursting in the water. Max is the first to notice another noise, quiet at first, but soon loud enough for him to ask a question.

'Why has my duck started ticking, Mum?'

~~~~

This is the first of many mysterious deaths around the world. In the same moment that neighbours are rushing to the scene of the explosion, a young man is jogging along Brighton Promenade. He sees something bright and yellow, sitting upright and smiling on the wet stones. Curiosity wins him over and he walks towards it. He picks it up and smiles as he sets off for home, already looking forward to sharing a bath with his partner and their new yellow friend.

NO DEPOSIT REQUIRED

In a large, white-walled room, twenty-three people are waiting for a presentation to begin. Two women, wearing identical powder blue trouser suits and fixed smiles, stand at the front next to a screen, displaying the words:

SPACE & TIME SHARE OFFER

One of the women noisily clears her throat. Once everyone is paying attention, the other starts to speak.

'Good afternoon, ladies and gentlemen, and thank you for coming along today. My name is Grace Tomori, and this is my colleague, Becca Sailstorfer.'

An unwanted interruption comes from the second row.

'They're unusual names.'
'Are they, Sir? I suppose they must be if you say so, but let's get back to why we're all here, shall we? Now, you've all read the information on our publicity literature that came with the invitation, yes?'

A low, affirmatory murmur ripples around the room.

'Wonderful, wonderful. I'll pass you over to Becca to tell you more about this once in a lifetime opportunity, and we truly mean that. Don't we, Becca?'
'We do indeed, Grace. Please turn your attention to the screen, everyone. This first image is one of our amazing properties. As you can see, it has a large swimming pool and is surrounded by a high fence for added security.'

A hand is raised towards the back of the room. Becca's smile nearly slips but she maintains her composure.

'The photograph looks lovely and the villa looks pretty impressive, but we can't see the surrounding neighbourhood. Why is that?'

Becca nervously looks at Grace, who quickly thinks on her paws and comes up with an answer.

'Well, Sir, that's because the property is situated in a very exclusive neighbourhood so we can't give too many details away during this presentation but, rest assured, you can be sure of a very special welcome if you decide to take up this incredible offer. Now I'll pass you back to Becca.'

'Thank you, Grace. If you all open your brochures at page seventeen, you'll find details of our pricing structure and....'

'Eeaaugh!'

'Is something the matter, Madam?'

'Something disgusting just fell out when I opened mine!'

Becca flashes a look at Grace, who rushes forwards to pick the item off the floor. It's a patch of dried human skin with several bite marks in it.

'I sincerely apologise, Madam. How did that get in there? Let's take a little break for you to get over the shock. Becca, I think this might be a good time to hand round the snacks.'

A little nod passes between the glamourous representatives. They pick up a bowl each and move among their guests, but the woman who found the piece of flesh declines.

'Thank you, but I'm really not very hungry, ladies.'
'But we insist! Don't we, Grace?'
'We do, Becca. Try one at least, Madam.'
'Oh.... very well.'

Grace and Becca return to their positions next to the large screen. They prattle on about the benefits of signing up early, all the while waiting for the strong sedatives to take effect. Sure enough, soon heads start to droop, the last succumbing midway through asking a question.

'Why is the company called 'SPACE & Time Sha.... Sha.... Sh....'
'You'll soon find out, Sir.'

With everyone in a deep sleep, Becca and Grace attach a transporter disc to the forehead of each victim. They watch the process of transference begin, and Becca compliments her colleague.

'Your idea of taking random names from human publications and splicing them together to create new ones was really clever.'
'Thank you, Becca. I think we'll use that technique from now on. *My* favourite moment is when they look at the ridiculously low figures in the brochure, not realising that everything is fake, and that they'll soon be paying a *very* different price! Human greed is so pathetic.'
'Speaking of greed, Grace, let's go and feast. All that fake smiling has made me ravenous!'

Becca and Grace place a disc on their own foreheads and laugh as they start to dissolve into the air, leaving the bland room behind.

~ ~ ~ ~

The humans regain consciousness at roughly the same time and drowsily take in their new surroundings. They are all sitting around the edge of a large swimming pool near an impressive villa which they recognise, but noises from the other side of the high fence transfer the scene from idyllic to disturbing.

Suddenly huge canine creatures bound over the wooden structure, whilst others leap from the villa windows, all landing on the broad, marble-effect patio. They survey the scene before them, running long blue tongues over sharp, yellowed fangs. The warm water quickly turns red and viscous, littered with shreds of clothing.

The last to arrive shed their powder blue trouser suits and dive into the pool, their grey and black striped fur soon matted with blood.

SAND WHERE IT SHOULDN'T BE

Barry and Brenda could hardly wait. The memories of that holiday in Torremolinos still shone as brightly as the Spanish sun, even though it happened in 1979. Donkey rides, melting ice creams, sea and sandcastles – everything had been perfect, so why not try to recreate that happy event?

~~~~

They weren't married at the time and had been 'courting' for just over two years. Barry and Brenda were crazy about each other and had excitedly told their respective parents about the holiday, although they weren't exactly truthful about their sleeping arrangements. Separate rooms had been booked, yes, but the couple had a rather different plan in mind.

An exhilarating sense of freedom rushed through them as the plane touched down. Brenda turned to Barry and saw a twinkle in his eyes. She smiled at him with the same sparkle and they both knew what it meant.

During the holiday, the couple were like excited children. Their days were filled with laughter and fun, heightened by the knowledge of what was to happen every night around midnight. Barry would wait outside Brenda's room, knock gently three times and wait for her to open the door. They would then hungrily embrace, eager to explore each other's bodies, but careful not to make too much noise. The sex was fantastic and surprised them both with its intensity. To avoid any unnecessary complications, Barry used protection, which eased Brenda's mind. He left her with a tender kiss each time, before creeping back to his room.

He asked for her hand in marriage on the last day over dinner, and she accepted without a moment's hesitation. Maybe it was the fact that their holiday was almost over, or maybe it was the sheer thrill of getting engaged. Either way, Barry and Brenda's lovemaking that night was explosive, to say the least.

During the first four years of wedlock, however, their passion gradually crumbled away like a sandcastle yielding to the tide. Their time in the bedroom, no longer steamy and driven by primal urges, settled into a bland nothingness, consisting of holding hands in silence before switching off the bedside lamps in unison. On several occasions, Barry tried to rekindle their sexual spark by reading erotic literature to Brenda by candlelight before they went to bed. He had found this to be deeply arousing, but every time Brenda merely drained her mug of cocoa, shrugged and climbed the stairs without him. It was only when she chanced upon an old photo album of that holiday together that things started to heat up again and now the day had come for their little adventure.

~~~~

The excited couple push the sofa and armchairs against the left-hand wall to make room for the paddling pool. Barry fetches the wheelbarrow full of sand and tips its contents onto the plastic sheeting (must protect that carpet – it was £12.99 a square metre!). Brenda sticks a selection of holiday snaps on the walls then places plastic palm trees in each corner, as Barry uses a foot pump to inflate the pool. She positions a large fabric-covered donkey, a souvenir from the original trip, in the middle of the room. Her husband fills the pool with a hose attached to the kitchen tap then erects the two deckchairs on the sand.

They close the curtains, switch on the angle poise lamp to represent the sun and strip off. Barry and Brenda put on their stripy sombreros and smile at each other, happy to see that holiday twinkle return in their eyes. Not for long, though.

'Haven't we forgotten something, Barry?'

'Oh yes – the ice cream cones! Don't worry, Bren, I'll get them.'

'Hurry back, my holiday hunk! I don't want to be kept waiting.'

'I will, my sexy senorita! I promise!'

Barry rushes into the kitchen and takes the tub of ice cream out of the freezer. Eager to return to Brenda, he hurriedly fills two cones with raspberry ripple. Not bothering to replace the tub, he goes back to the living room and finds Brenda languishing seductively, or as seductively as possible, in one of the deck chairs.

'Here you are, gorgeous! Look what I've got for.... oh-ooh-oh!'

Barry trips over the donkey and falls, sending both scoops of ice cream into the air. They both land on Brenda's chest, the shock of the sudden cold making her scream out loud. She leaps up from the deckchair but loses her footing on the 'beach'. Desperate to help, Barry tries to stand, but only succeeds in falling on top of her. The ensuing struggle results in the paddling pool tipping over, sending water everywhere, including under the plastic sheeting. Tearful and covered in wet sand and gritty ice cream, Brenda hurls away her sombrero, runs upstairs and slams the bedroom door. Barry, as on so many occasions, sits alone in the living room and wonders where it all went wrong.

~~~~

'Bren? Brenda, love? I've cleaned up downstairs and everything's nearly back to normal. There's only the carpet to dry out and that shouldn't take too long.'

Still wearing his sombrero, Barry climbs into bed next to Brenda and gently places the hat he's brought upstairs on her turned-away head. She moves to face him and they both start to laugh, then Barry's expression becomes serious.

'Let's face it, Mrs. Stevens. A memory should remain exactly that - a memory. It's impossible to capture something that's already gone, and we were fools to try it.'

'Agreed, Mr. Stevens, and we'll always have those photographs to remind us. Now, how about getting another two raspberry ripples?'

'Only if I get a long, slow cuddle first!'

Barry and Brenda laugh as they take off their slightly ridiculous hats, throw them onto the carpet and slide under the duvet.

VOWEL MOVEMENT

'The Five' are holding an urgent meeting at The Alphabet Club, a run-down dive on the fringes of town. They sit in the shadowy gloom in silence, three not knowing how to process the new information and the other two defiant and resolute. One of the confused trio eventually speaks.

'What do you mean, you want to leave the group?'
'It's perfectly straightforward. We just want to be together, that's all.'
'But you can't! It'll change everything forever! Things just won't make any sense if you go.'
'We've considered that, I, but our decision is final. You three will just have to manage without us.'

The one with the round face and a constant look of surprise is the next to challenge the pair.

'Your reasoning doesn't make sense! I can think of dozens of examples where you sit side by side. For example, ChauffEUr, MusEUm, SabotEUr....'
'Appropriate under the circumstances, that last one, O.'

Anger grew in I on hearing that remark.

'AmatEUr sarcasm – that's all I'd expect from U! Besides, what the dEUce did you think our reaction would be? EUphoria? Without you two, the whole language will be rendered completely ineffective.'

The renegade couple start to giggle, but soon stop when A stands up, imposing and angry.

'What's so funny?'
'Er.... the thought of you three suddenly becoming EUnuchs, nEUtered and slightly ridiculous.'

'Oh, please! Can't you think of a better EUphemism than that?'

This makes the couple burst out laughing, but then E nudges U and they regain their composure, both recognising the seriousness of the situation.

'Look. We don't mean to cause a fEUd and we're not manoEUvering to get special treatment, but the three of you are being a bit nEUrotic about all this. Of course, any great change can cause anxiety, but don't get so stressed about it!'

'I suppose you'll just swan off somewhere cool and detached, with a false sense of grandEUr.'

'Quite frankly, I, that's none of your business, but who knows? We might end up as entreprenEUrs. I'm sure there would be a veritable qUEUE beating a path to our door before long.'

'That's my favourite word, E. We're together twice in that one.'

'I know, U sweet thing. I love it too.'

A summons O and I to stand, before addressing the duo.

'Very well. It is clear you can't be persuaded to stay. Even though you have no interest in the chaos that your departure will cause, I must say we will be sorry to see you go. You have both been vital parts of this team and your work has been exemplary and....'

'Oh, spare us the EUlogy! Come on, we're off. Take a closEUp look at yourselves, you three! Pathetic!'

So it was that th writt n word was chang d for v r. Som books still got p blish d b t, grad ally, adaptations w r bro ght in and th missing vow ls w r r plac d.

Thankfvlly, 3v3rything tvrn3d ovt w3ll in th3 3nd, as yov can s33.

THE GIFT THAT KEEPS ON GIVING

Martha traced an arc with her left glove on the steamed-up glass and peered out through the bus window. Another disappointing Valentine's Day evening lurked ahead, mocking her and stabbing at her loneliness. No cards, gifts or flowers ever arrived at her door on this date, and she had no reason to hope that this one would be any different.

Martha had always loathed February. January was bad enough, but at least there wasn't too great a risk of snow in the first month of the year, unlike now. Several inches had fallen during the day, and she stared up at the cotton wool-like flakes as they drifted down from a darkened sky, mesmerised by their slow trajectories.

Martha wearily turned away from the window and was surprised to find a strange item on the seat beside her. She gazed at the heart-shaped box, shaded a brilliant scarlet with a pink ribbon and bow attached diagonally across the flat surface. The gaudy colours seemed completely at odds with the end-of-week greyness outside and the threadbare seat upon which it sat. Martha cast a nervous glance at the other passengers, but no-one seemed to have noticed it at all.

Questions raced through her mind, in the same way that buses used to turn up in threes. Who had left the box there? Why had it been abandoned and, most importantly, who was the intended recipient?

Martha noticed a piece of white card tucked under the ribbon and removed it for closer inspection. It carried the words 'TO' and 'FROM' in a swirling font that was far too fussy for *her* taste, but nothing else was written there.

Martha was just about to slide the card back into position when she saw her own name scratchily appearing next to the word 'TO', although the 'FROM' line remained resolutely blank. Intrigued, she thrust both box and card into her bag. Martha looked up and realised that the next stop was hers. She pressed the bell in good time, already looking forward to further investigation of the package when she got home.

~~~~

Martha managed to quell her curiosity until she had finished her evening meal. She took the box through to the sitting room and placed it on the coffee table, eager to look inside. After all, it was addressed to *her*, wasn't it? The bow and ribbon detached easily, and Martha gingerly lifted the heart-shaped lid. She was amazed at what she found inside.

In front of her sat a single chocolate heart, about twenty-five centimetres from top to base, nestling in a black ruffled lining. Her name was etched deeply into its surface with a display of hearts and stars surrounding all six letters. Martha removed the sweet from the box and realised that it must be hollow, judging by its insubstantial weight. She turned the confectionery upside down to examine it for further markings, but there were none, so instead Martha contemplated the pleasurable experience that awaited her.

She struck the unexpected gift against the edge of the table and it broke into two equal parts. Martha took a tentative bite and discovered that it was the best chocolate she had ever tasted, not oversweet and wonderfully smooth. Initially intending to only eat one half, Martha quickly lost all sense of willpower and consumed the whole lot by the end of the evening. Feeling more than a little guilty, she took the box and lid through to the kitchen for recycling and left them on the draining board before going to bed.

Next morning, Martha entered the kitchen with a stretch and a yawn, fully rested after a satisfying sleep. She rubbed her eyes in disbelief, however, when she saw the box with the lid freshly secured and newly tied and bowed with the pink sash.

Confused and convinced that she'd left the ribbon on the coffee table last night, Martha untied it again and slowly lifted the bright red lid. In astonishment, she found another chocolate beneath, identical to the first and just as appealing. Thank goodness it was the weekend, she thought. With no need to step out in the snow, Martha realised that she could just gorge herself on more of the excellent chocolate, already believing that the box would keep replenishing its contents as soon as it was empty.

This indeed proved to be the case. To her delight and surprise, Martha never gained weight over the weeks and months that followed. She decided that this must be due to some strange ingredient in the mix, but occasionally wondered if the chocolate itself was as lonely as she was and found comfort in her continuing indulgence.

Inevitably, Valentine's Day came around again, but this time Martha just didn't care. As she lifted a fresh chocolate from the scarlet box that evening, she finally understood that the time-consuming, trap-laden pursuit of love isn't worth the effort or heartache.

Martha smiled and made a personal proclamation out loud. No-one was there to hear it, which didn't bother her in the slightest:

'Chocolate doesn't forget your birthday. It doesn't lie or cheat on you and it doesn't judge or criticise. What chocolate *does* do is give you a warm hug on a certain night in February, and that's *all I need.*'

A SURFACING OF REGRET

I never looked back. Even after my most brutal assignments, when my clients asked me to engage in extreme torture before the eventual kill, I would just walk away. Being the consummate professional, I'd make sure there wasn't any incriminating evidence left at the scene, unless I was framing someone else, of course. Apart from that I'd just go home, put my blood-stained clothes in the wash and relax with a whisky. I enjoyed making my 'customers' wait before I made the phone call, confirming that their wishes had been carried out successfully. It didn't matter who they were, obscenely rich idiots or middle-ranking businessmen. Why shouldn't they squirm a little? After all, I'd done their dirty work for them and I revelled in those brief moments of power.

I never liked the term 'hit man'. I hated people using that lazy definition, because it always struck me as rather vague and didn't describe my specific set of work skills properly. I mean, anyone can hit someone, male or female, young or old. No, what *I* provided was a bespoke, contract killing service, discreet and efficient.

My favourite jobs? Well, two spring to mind.

I was particularly proud of the Johnson Brothers brief. They were notorious criminals, with fingers in far too many pies. Some of those pies were a bit too hot to handle, if you know what I mean. It was a pleasure to set them against each other in that warehouse. All I had to do was circulate rumours in the criminal fraternity that each was having an affair with the other's wife. At the height of the argument, I just calmly stepped out of my hiding place and shot them. Both women were my clients on that one, and they tipped me off as to where the men were going to 'sort things out'. Those ladies had suffered all kinds of abuse at the hands of their 'loving husbands' over several years, including black eyes after the brothers first heard the gossip on the street, so it felt good to mete out that kind of justice for them. They paid well, too.

The other job was of a kind that doesn't come along too often. The man who hired me was the owner of a supermarket in a town barely big enough to have two such stores. There was only a brief conversation between us on my private number, the words of my would-be client whispered, but tinged with hatred.

'I want you to get rid of my rival. Since he set up in business, he's stolen most of my customers. I don't care how you do it.... please just do it.'

Music to my ears, that. I'm a man of imagination, you see, so an open brief sets my mind racing. Earlier in the week I'd driven past the store, noted the name on the alarm cover then mocked up a convincing ID card and badge of the security company. On the day of the job I went in during the afternoon, pretending to be there to service the surveillance equipment. I left after setting the system to fail from 6.00 p.m. onwards, then waited until all his staff had gone home.

I caught him by surprise as he was locking up. Killing him was straightforward enough – single bullet, you know the sort of thing – but then my creativity kicked in as I dragged his body back inside.

I made a tall stack of sturdy plastic shopping baskets, tied my victim to them, then started to circle him with the first tins of baked beans. I soon discovered that there weren't enough tins on the shelves, but I found several packs of them in the storeroom. As the tower grew the process became easier, although I had to use a step ladder to complete my work. I loved the whole retro feel of this one, imagining the customers' faces as they withdrew the cans, innocently making the gradual reveal. Classic.

~~~~

I know, I know – I told you that I never looked back. Well, I didn't, not until last night, when I became the one to be 'hit'. The victim of my own success? Probably. Someone clearly planned this revenge attack thoroughly, luring me to a clandestine meeting that turned out to be a lie.

So now I sit here in complete darkness, tightly bound, blindfolded and gagged. All I can hear is muffled laughter from the next room. My fate is in the hands of others now, so all I can do is await my own death.

I don't know exactly how long I've been here but *do* know that it's given me time to reflect on my 'work'. I've brought pain and suffering to my victims' families and friends, clinging on in their grief to cherished memories. I realise now that I coldly ruined so many lives, and for that I have just one word to say:

Sorry.

WE ARE THE MENU

The scene is set in a far from exclusive restaurant, as it could be any of us. On a patch of human skin, we find two hungry diners being greeted by a rather obsequious waiter.

'Good evening, Sir. Madam. Are you both ready to order?'

'Well, everything in our section on the menu looks so delicious it's hard to choose. Do you have any suggestions?'

'Of course, Madam. If I might suggest a starter of small scalp flakes followed by another selection of scalp flakes, only this time in assorted sizes to make for a more interesting dining experience.'

'Are they freshly picked?'

'Why yes, Sir. They were harvested this very morning and have been brought quite a long way for your delectation and delight.'

'That all sounds wonderful, so I think we'll go with your recommendations. Tell me, why *is* the menu divided like that?'

'As I'm sure you can appreciate, we have a rather diverse clientele here, Sir. Every diner has most particular tastes, so it just makes everything easier for all concerned if the menu is laid out in such a fashion. Now if you will excuse me, I need to attend to other guests.'

A large gnat has landed near the head lice and is standing motionless.

'If you would like to make yourself comfortable, Madam. Is there any particular area of the restaurant on which you would like to feast?'

'No, I'm fine here, thank you.'

'Very good, Madam. I see you've brought your own straw, as always.'

Next a group of bed bugs approach the waiter. They huddle together as he turns to address them collectively.

'Good evening, good evening! If you'd all like to take a space over.... here, you can start your meal immediately. Oh, and if any of you nymphs feel a need to shed your skins again, don't worry. We can sweep them up and use them as a garnish tomorrow.'

The waiter sees a heavily pregnant scabies mite shuffling into view. She faces him directly then asks a rather urgent question.

'Is the skin thin around here?'
'Well, Madam, if you keep moving in *that* direction, I know there's an expanse that will suit your requirements perfectly.'
'Wonderful. It just makes everything easier for me, that's all. There's nothing I enjoy more than a good burrowing.'
'I fully understand, Madam. By the way, if you have an urgent desire to lay your eggs as you feed, please do so. We can send your young on to you after hatching.'
'I can feel it won't be long now! Thank you so much.'
'Not at all, Madam, not at all.'

Suddenly a group of boisterous adult fleas bounce in, pinging around everywhere and disturbing some of the diners. The waiter politely but firmly asserts his authority.

'You are all most welcome to join us, but might I respectfully request that you each find a place to settle for a few moments? This is a popular place to feed, so please respect the other diners as you begin to take your fill.'

No-one has spoken to them in such a manner since they were larvae. Suitably chastened, they stand still and lower their mouth parts, with only three of them daring to look at the waiter.

Half an hour later, he moves across to the head lice, now fully replete, as they prepare to leave.

'I trust you both had an enjoyable evening.'
'Oh, yes! We just said that we couldn't manage another flake!'
'I'm delighted to hear it, Madam.'
'There was one thing, though.'
'Yes?'
'We were wondering what that soothing music was, playing in the background as we ate.'
'The music, Sir? Oh, that was a selection of songs by Gnat King Cole!'

A DEEP DEPRESSION MOVES IN

'Now it's time to find out about the weather from Anna Chambers.'

You can get through this. You CAN get through this. You MUST get through this.

A pause.

'Anna?'

'Oh, sorry, Steve. Yes, well, with high pressure still firmly in charge, we're all in for a sunny Saturday and, if anything, Sunday will be just that little bit warmer.'

Keep going. Just keep going.

Another pause, and this one was long enough to cause presenters Steve and Julie to shuffle uncomfortably on the sofa. Martin, the programme's producer, bit his lip and tried to stay calm.

'....and how are things shaping up for next week, Anna? Anna?'

Silence and a blank expression. Anna had tried, she'd really tried to focus on her three-minute slot next to the weather chart, desperately forcing down the emotional turmoil within her, but it had ultimately proved impossible. Why did Dan storm out in a rage just after midnight, and where had all those hurtful accusations come from? It was a bit rich of him to say that *she* was having an affair (she wasn't), when she knew he was guilty of the same charge.

Anna's thoughts became increasingly troubled, and she wondered how she would explain to her parents that the planned weekend visit would not now take place. Should she be honest about Dan's departure, or try to fashion a convincing lie? Mum and Dad were so proud of her television career and she knew that they would be watching her now, a fact that made this whole situation much worse.

'Anna? Are you alright over there?'

Fix the smile and keep going. No! I can't! I CAN'T!

Anna stood frozen to the spot and closed her eyes. She vaguely heard Steve and Julie thanking her before closing the programme, but then a disturbing image sprang into her anxious mind.

~~~~

She was standing in her usual position on set, but the weather map showed a very different country now. The familiar outline of the British Isles had been replaced by another easily recognised form. The new land mass was heart-shaped, but the coastline was dramatically rugged, with the internal terrain mountainous and unwelcoming. Anna was facing the camera as usual, but her fists were clenched in anger over Dan's behaviour. This was completely out of character and something she would never normally do, or be allowed to do, on screen.

She stared at the monitor in front of her and was surprised to see a growing turbulence developing there. Isobars had started to bunch tightly together across the centre of the heart, and exclamatory weather warnings appeared in three places. The wind speeds in their little arrowed circles were rapidly increasing, and quickly rose to dangerous, 'high risk of damage' levels. Anna watched as the temperature plummeted to zero and realised that she was looking at a map of her own emotional disturbance. She started to cry and, in that same moment, an electric blue swathe of rain, punctuated by flashes of green and yellow, swept across her own personal landscape.

Anna was further upset to find raindrops mingling with her tears and splashing onto the studio floor. A light breeze touched her shoulders (1-5 km/hr), before swiftly moving through gentle (12-19) to moderate (20-28). A sense of deep unease rose within her, matching the increasing wind speeds. When fresh status (29-38) was reached, Anna felt distinctly uncomfortable, and hugged herself tightly. It was only then that she realised she was naked, the bitter, acidic rain of her unhappiness having dissolved her clothes clean away and further heightening her sense of vulnerability. The wind rapidly surged through numbers 6 to 9 on the Beaufort scale, achieving strong gale level within minutes.

Anna, crumpled and defeated, lay down on the floor amongst the spreading puddles. The wind whipped and whirled above her, now at storm level (103-117). She curled her rain-soaked body into a foetal position and howled into the terrifying turbulence. Shivering wildly in the cold and wet, she felt compelled to look at the weather map behind her. Anna watched in horror as the island of her heart split in two, then slowly sank into the swirling dark waters. All was lost in this distressing vision. She was completely alone in what was now a full hurricane (117+), lightning flashes intermittently illuminating the scene.

~~~~

In the *real* world, Steve and Julie were trying to speak to Anna, but she remained motionless and incommunicative. Martin angrily rushed on to the set and let rip with a few expletives. He soon realised, however, that shouting and screaming abuse were not going to achieve anything and all three moved away. Camera crew and other staff also left Anna alone, unsure what to do next.

Anna Chambers, popular TV weather presenter, slowly opened her eyes and looked around the studio. She felt an enormous surge of relief, knowing that the windswept, naked nightmare was over, whilst recognising that real life held little comfort now. Her career was probably dead, and her marriage certainly was. She walked past the large cameras, leaving the unforgiving, fast-moving world of television behind.

TIME TO LEAVE: 1

A beautiful spring morning. The air is alive with a heady mix of fragrances and everywhere there are blossoms bursting forth and birds singing. Amidst this serenity, however, there is a scene of familial strife.

'Feed me! Feed me! Come on! Feed me!'
'But you've only just finished the breakfast I brought you earlier. You can't still be hungry!'
'Well, I am. You said yourself that I'm a growing lad and, as a parent, it's your duty to make sure I get enough to eat.'
'Alright, alright. I'll see what I can find, but I have to tell you that I've become completely exhausted with all this rushing around after you.'
'Not really my problem. Now, off you go!'

She sets off again and the pampered child watches her leave. Whilst alone, he aimlessly looks around with nothing better to do, but starts to shuffle eagerly in his bed when he sees her returning.

'You took your time, I must say! What have you got for me? Quick! Show me!'
'Anyone would think you hadn't eaten for weeks, boy! Here you are....'

Without a word of thanks or appreciation for his mother's efforts, the overweight brat snatches at the food and swallows it in one go.

'I suppose that will do for now. Er.... why don't you take a little rest, hmm? Besides, Mum, I've got something to tell you.'

He cocks his head on one side and pauses before addressing her further, eager to drop his emotional bombshell.

'What is it, son? Have I done something to upset you?'

'No, no, this isn't about anything you've done. It's all about me, like everything else around here, in case you hadn't noticed. You see, and I really hate having to tell you this, but you're not my real mother.'

'But your father and I raised you as our own! Haven't we provided all the food you've ever wanted and given you a nice place to live?'

'Yeah, and I appreciate all that but.... well.... it's time for me to leave. Today. Now.'

'Why, you ungrateful child! Just wait until your father hears about this!'

'Whatever. Breaking news! He's not my real dad, so I couldn't care less. I'll be off, then. Bye!'

With that, the young adult leaves his weary, confused carer behind and doesn't look back. Instead he pauses a short distance away from the 'family home', listens to the sounds of spring and lets out a single cry:

'CUCKOO!'

TIME TO LEAVE: 2

Alex quietly sets his large sports bag down near the front door. He pauses for a moment, then walks from the hall to the kitchen, where Paula is washing up after breakfast. He clears his throat which, as intended, gets her attention and she turns to face him.

'Hello, love. Do you need anything?'
'No, thanks. Everything's fine, but....'
'Yes?'
'It's just that, well.... Mum, I've got something to tell you.'

His mother notices his serious expression, so slowly puts down the plate she was drying and tries hard to steady herself for the revelation to come. Alex opens his mouth to speak, but he is immediately silenced by Paula's fears, tumbling from her lips and filling the small kitchen.

'I've been dreading this moment, Alex, let me tell you. I've thought for some time that there was something you were keeping from me and your father. I mean, you never have any of your college friends over and we both think you spend far too much time in your room. Have you been gambling online up there? Is that it? It's a complete mug's game, Alex, you know I'm right! You'd better come clean. Exactly how much money have you wasted?

'Or perhaps you're gay. If so, well, I'm disappointed that we won't have any grandchildren running around the place, but I'm more concerned about how your father will take the news, to be honest. You *know* how he reacts to things like that on the television. Oh dear, and what will the neighbours think?

'Or have you got some young woman pregnant? You know I've always disapproved of sex before marriage and Dad feels the same way, so don't expect any sympathy from us if that's the case. You're on your own there. 'Drugs? Is it drugs? Didn't we bring you up to resist that sort of temptation? I suppose your college mates think it's 'cool', or whatever the phrase is these days. Even if you manage to free yourself from it, I'll always be afraid that you'll start up again! Oh, and don't think that alcohol is any less addictive. Are you a secret drinker? Is that what you want to tell me, Alex? Please, son! Just tell me!'

Alex stares at his mother in silence. Devastated and disappointed by what he has just heard, the eighteen-year-old takes a deep breath before responding.

'Mum, what I wanted to tell you was how much I love you and Dad, and how painful it is for me to move out today. I've thought long and hard about this difficult decision but, quite frankly, having heard you spout all those outdated attitudes, I've realised that I'm definitely doing the right thing.'
'Wait, Alex! I didn't mean....'
'Yes, you did, Mum! You've clearly been keeping those poisonous, selfish thoughts inside for some time, so don't try to deny it! Fuck! I can't wait to get away from here.'

Alex leaves the kitchen but stops in the doorway. He turns to face his mother one last time.

'So that you know, two items on your little list *do* apply to me, but you'll just have to guess which ones, won't you? I'm off!'

Alex storms down the hall and picks up his sports bag. He opens the front door, takes one last look around and slams it shut behind him.

Paula returns to the sink with the noise reverberating in her ears and stares at the remaining soap bubbles. She watches as they burst and disappear into nothing, aided now by her sorry tears. After a few minutes, she raises her head and looks out of the kitchen window, wondering how she will tell her husband what has happened. She also wonders where Alex will be sleeping tonight.

SOMETHING FISHY

Gustav hated Anton from the moment he stepped into what he regarded as 'his' kitchen. He had been Head Chef at 'Le Saumon' for nearly five years now and took pride in receiving excellent feedback from both clientele and management. Even the critics had treated him well, often tripping over superlatives to praise his dishes. The downside of his success was that interest in the restaurant had risen exponentially. As a result, with 'Le Saumon' fully booked for several months ahead, the owner had deemed it necessary to employ an Executive Chef to assist the maestro.

It was little things at first. Anton would taste Gustav's food without being asked, and then deliver his unwanted feedback:

'I bow to your superior culinary expertise, of course, but if I might suggest.... perhaps a little more paprika in your bouillabaisse?'

Or:

'Gustav, *Gustav*. You know how I respect you and your fully deserved reputation, but this lobster bisque.... well, it just seems rather lacking in flavour. I hope you don't mind me saying.'

Worst of all was the critique of Gustav's signature dish, Bourride with Lemon Aioli. Perfected during his career, it soon became a constant on 'Le Saumon's menu. The halibut had to be cooked to perfection and the stew flavoured with exactly the right amount of fennel before Gustav would even consider bringing it to the pass, so when Anton described the seasoning as 'mediocre', well, everything went downhill from there.

The atmosphere felt thick with hatred on every subsequent service, with barely a civil word uttered between them. Gustav vented his anger on assorted crustacea, aggressively cracking open lobster and crab shells, swearing under his breath as he did so. Junior staff tried their best to keep out of his way, almost impossible in the circumstances, but then the claims of sabotage started.

Gustav began accusing Anton of throwing fragments of shell or handfuls of salt into his creations, just after the Head Chef had taste-checked the dishes and before waiting staff served them to 'Le Saumon's discerning customers. Anton would just shrug and smirk which infuriated Gustav still further. Everyone in the kitchen became used to this heightened tension, but neither staff nor management expected to see Anton writhing in agony on the tiled floor during this lunchtime's service. No-one defended Gustav as he was led away by two uniformed officers, his protests of innocence falling on deaf ears, including mine.

Me? Who am *I*? My name's Marie and I've worked at 'Le Saumon' for.... let me see now.... sixteen months. I enjoyed working here at first, but then Gustav started making lewd suggestions and deliberately pushing against me as I prepped the veg for each service. Why didn't I say anything? What, and get the sack? No-one would have believed a lowly commis chef like me, anyway. When Anton started giving me the same unwanted attention, however, I knew things had to change around here.

How did he die? Simple, really. I just waited for Anton to ask for a spoon to check his seasoning and passed him the one I'd prepared. The viscous, tasteless poison started to take effect the moment he swallowed the food sample, and he was dead within two minutes. Everyone was screaming in the kitchen, so I joined in to cover my tracks.

Those bastards got what they deserved, and I served up a plate of the finest red herrings during my police interview, all innocence and subterfuge. Now, if you'll excuse me – I must get on with my food prep for this evening. They've managed to draft in a chef from another restaurant for now, so I'm keen to make a good impression. Who knows? Might be a promotion in it if I play my cards right. After all, it's hard to find reliable and honest staff these days, isn't it?

ADVERTISEMENT

NEW BUT LIMITED STOCK AVAILABLE NOW. ONCE THEY'RE GONE, THEY'RE GONE!

SPECIES NUMBER 498326532. HOMO SAPIENS (EARTH) - MALE OR FEMALE. ONLY ADULT FORMS AVAILABLE. USAGES: ENSLAVEMENT, CURIOSITY VALUE, LIVE MEAT. INCLUDED IN PRICE: EMOTION ADAPTER – OFFERS YOU THE ABILITY TO CHANGE HUMAN EMOTIONS. WATCH THEM MOVE THROUGH A RANGE FROM JOY TO DEPRESSION FOR YOUR OWN AMUSEMENT. EARLY PURCHASERS HAVE REPORTED HIGH LEVELS OF PLEASURE AS THEY OBSERVED HUMAN FACES SHOWING CURIOSITY, PAIN, ABJECT FEAR, ETC.

PLEASE SPECIFY GENDER AT CHECKOUT. ALL METHODS OF PAYMENT ACCEPTED. PLEASE USE UNIVERSAL CURRENCY CONVERTER ON PAYMENT PAGE.

DISCLAIMER: HUMANS MAY BE DISORIENTED WHEN THEY FIRST SEE THEIR NEW ENVIRONMENT BUT, ONCE THEY REALISE THERE IS NO ESCAPE, THIS SHOULD SOON PASS.

HUMANS ARE PARTICULARLY STUPID. GIVEN THE CHANCE, THEY WILL RUIN THEIR ENVIRONMENT OR FIGHT EACH OTHER TO THE DEATH OVER PETTY DIFFERENCES. UNLESS KEPT UNDER CLOSE SUPERVISION OR RESTRAINT, YOUR HUMAN MAY BECOME UNSTABLE AS THEY HAVE A HISTORY OF DESTRUCTIVE BEHAVIOUR, THEREFORE NO RETURNS WILL BE ACCEPTED UNDER ANY CIRCUMSTANCES. YOUR HUMAN WILL BE DISPATCHED WITH LIFE SUPPORT APPARATUS INCLUDED IN THE PACKAGING AND SHOULD REACH YOU IN PERFECT CONDITION. NO

LIABILITY WILL BE ACCEPTED FOR ANY DAMAGE CAUSED DURING TRANSIT - BRUISING, BROKEN BONES, ETC. - AS YOUR PURCHASE WILL HAVE TRAVELLED A GREAT DISTANCE TO FULFIL YOUR ORDER.

IT IS STRONGLY SUGGESTED THAT YOU PLACE YOUR ORDER WITHOUT DELAY BECAUSE THERE ARE LIMITED SUPPLIES OF THIS ITEM, DUE TO GLOBAL CONFLICT ON THEIR HOME PLANET, BUT SALVAGE WILL CONTINUE TO SECURE FURTHER STOCK FOR A SHORT PERIOD. POTENTIAL CUSTOMERS MUST ACCEPT THAT *THESE* HUMANS MIGHT BE DAMAGED IN SOME WAY, BUT THEY WILL BE OFFERED AT A REDUCED RATE AS A RESULT. THESE ITEMS WILL NOT BE SOLD AS FOOD, UNLESS YOU STATE IN YOUR ORDER THAT YOUR RACE IS UNAFFECTED BY IRRADIATED MEAT.

IRONING BORED

Lift item out of basket. Iron item. Fold item. Place item in ironed pile. Lift item out of basket. Iron item. Fold item. Place item in ironed pile. Lift item out of basket. Iron item. Fold item. Place item in ironed pile. LIFT. IRON. FOLD. PLACE. LIFT. IRON. FOLD. PLACE. LIFT. IRON. FOLD. PLACE.

Malcolm yawns and looks through his French windows to the small garden beyond. The mindless task has stolen over an hour of his day off already, and he hasn't even noticed that the mid-morning rain has stopped. He wearily inspects the laundry basket. Only one more shirt to iron then he is done for another week.

Most of his shirts are white, but he owns a couple that are marginally more interesting. One is a very subtle pink, the other a pale shade of lavender, and it is the latter that awaits his attention.

LIFT. IRON. FOLD. PLACE.

But wait. There is something else in the bottom of the basket. Malcolm had completely forgotten the tablecloth, especially as he considered throwing it away after the dinner party last weekend. It was a present from his sister, brought back from a holiday in Malta several years ago, but he never liked it much. The colours are too bright and the patterning too strong for his liking. Now, as he drapes it over the ironing board, he realises how little Sarah knows him or his personal taste.

His ex-girlfriend Magda had sworn that the spillage was an accident, but Malcolm wasn't so sure (why had he invited *her* anyway?). He is pleased to find that the gazpacho stain has completely disappeared, and that the colours have held fast, for he had taken a risk putting it in with his shirts. Malcolm resigns himself to the fact that he will have to keep the thing, albeit stored in a bottom drawer out of sight. He had only used it on Saturday because Sarah had been persuaded to come, although she had cancelled the day before, due to her son being ill.

The gaudy tablecloth completely covers the board's surface. Malcolm lifts the iron and is amazed when something extraordinary happens. The slightly crinkled fabric lifts itself up and hovers in mid-air, rippling gently. It appears to wait impatiently whilst the ironing board packs its legs away underneath and joins it, floating above the carpet. This achieved, the tablecloth wraps itself tightly around the folded structure. Still holding the iron, Malcolm stands stock still, anxious as to what might happen next.

The now highly patterned object turns to 'face' him, the bluntly pointed end dipping up and down as if expecting a particular response. When the thing spins back to its original position and gently nudges him, Malcolm realises that he is being prompted to climb aboard, so to speak. He hurriedly unplugs the iron, then places it upright on the wooden floor to cool down. The ironing board lowers itself slightly to offer further encouragement, at which point Malcolm throws caution to the wind. As he gingerly kneels on the board, he acknowledges just how out of character this behaviour is, but smiles, just the same.

When Malcolm is completely settled, the tablecloth-covered ironing board rears back, then hurtles through the French windows without warning, leaving splintered glass and wood in its wake. Malcolm laughs with child-like glee as he brushes raindrops from his clothes, dislodged from the trees as they climb ever skyward. He knows not where they are headed and cares even less. Malcolm lets out a jubilant scream of freedom as they rise together into the blue and away, away from drudgery!

WHITEOUT

The fifth cup of coffee? The sixth? Paul had lost count and it was only mid-morning. The blankness continued to mock him, and he slammed his fists down hard on the desk in sheer frustration.

Paul had never experienced writer's block before. Usually ideas for stories just seemed to flood out of him, so he found this new situation deeply unsettling. He drained his cup, went through to the lounge, and switched on the television. Paul found nothing to inspire him as he flicked through the channels, the final straw being a so-called celebrity droning on about her latest recording ('I've actually given 150% on this album and quite literally put my heart and soul into it, which I think makes it extremely unique'). He pressed the 'off' button and went back to his study.

Instead of facing the unforgiving whiteness on screen, Paul looked around the walls of the small room. Photographs of him receiving awards for his children's books at various ceremonies smiled down, but they all seemed to be of someone else who *looked* like him. In amongst these was a framed print of a front cover illustration, and it was this image that had graced his most famous work.

'The Crocodile's Birthday' had been an instant hit with both children and adults and had definitely 'put him on the map'. Although subsequent books were successful, none of them quite received the same level of adulation. Paul smiled, trying to imagine how many bookshelves still contained a copy of 'The Crocodile's Birthday', but then he looked down at his computer and reality kicked in again.

Staring at the white space, he remembered a Christmas card a friend had sent him once. The caption had read 'WHITE CAT ASLEEP IN A SNOWSTORM', but there was no image to accompany it. Perhaps not the greatest joke, but one that might just have saved Paul Forester's reputation. He set to work immediately and finished the first chapter by lunchtime:

THE JOURNEY THROUGH THE SNOW

CHAPTER ONE

'Are we nearly there yet, Peter? I'm so cold!'
Peter the white peacock shook his long tail feathers and stared at Freddie. 'I thought Arctic foxes were used to the snow. You live in it all the time, unlike me.'

'I do too, Peter,' said Patrick the Polar bear, 'but I agree with Freddie. It's really cold, even for me, and the snow is falling so thick and fast I can't tell where the sky meets the ground.'

'Oh, do stop moaning!' said Christina, a fluffy white Persian cat. 'We haven't any choice but to carry on! Besides, I'm enjoying swishing my long tail through the soft snow that's already settled, so *I'm* happy.'

'We'll fly ahead and see if we can find anything to suggest that we're getting close.'

Del and Delia, a pair of white doves, rose into the air and were soon lost from view.

'I hope they bring back good news, everyone,' said Ronald the white rabbit.

'I'm sure they will,' squeaked Martina, a little white mouse with long whiskers.

Henry the white hare let Martina climb up onto his back, realising that such a small animal must find battling the snow very tiring.

'Don't worry, little one, it can't be long now. We've been travelling for ages and I'm sure we'll be able to rest soon.'

Everyone looked up when the doves returned, but they had no real news for the party.

43

'All we saw was more deep snow, I'm afraid, Henry.'

'Never mind, Delia. At least we know what we have to face for a while.'

A silence, soft as the falling flakes, fell on the travellers. It was broken by Henry, who always tried to see the best in things.

'I know we're all really tired, but when we get there it will all be worth it, I promise. So come on, everybody, let's keep going!'

Feeling much more positive, Paul made a cheese and pickle sandwich and returned to his computer. At this point, he hadn't decided why the white animals were trekking through the snow or where they were headed, but he was confident these details would soon come to him. The main thing was that the pack ice of his writer's block had started to split and fall away, and in its wake a story had, at last, emerged.

Paul finished his lunch and decided that 'The Journey through the Snow' would include blank pages throughout the book instead of illustrations, encouraging children to either imagine the creatures or find out about them with their parents online. He would insist on these details when he met his publisher and smiled at the thought of Caroline's astonished face when he told her. He would, however, explain that these imaginary animals were all heading away from the reader, so no eyes, beaks, feet or paws would be seen anyway.

Paul Forester, happily back in the game, pushed his empty plate to one side and settled down to an afternoon of intense creativity with his new group of animal friends. They would all look after each other and get through the bleak whiteness together.

WHICH WITCH IS WHICH?

'Psst! Come in here and hide! Quick!'

The little frog peered into the shadowed space between the large bushes and could just make out several pairs of panic-filled eyes staring back at him. Well, not exactly *pairs* of eyes....

'Hide? From what?'

No-one answered, but something sticky landed on his head and pulled him into a place of darkness. Once inside, the toad released the small creature from his tongue's gluey grip and spoke in a whisper.

'Right, little one, don't make a sound! You should be safe with us for now, but nothing is for certain around here anymore. Not since *she* got her own television programme.'

'Who did, and what's a television programme?'

'Well, it all looks a bit crazy from in here. At first, we thought she'd completely lost it, talking to herself all the time. I mean, she's always been a bit, you know, odd, but then we heard these people chatting in there about this programme thingy. They were telling her how everyone will be curious and disgusted when they watch it, and that's when the terrible things started to happen.'

'What terrible things?'

'The recipes! The endless recipes!'

'I don't mean to sound stupid, but what's a recipe?'

The young amphibian looked so innocent, wide-eyed and wet around the earholes. The toad didn't want to tell him about the perils of this place, but felt he had no choice. He beckoned to a quartet of fireflies to shed a little light on the dreadful situation, thinking that 'show' was better than 'tell' any day.

The frog's mouth dropped open with shock as he looked around the small dim space. In the barely lit gloom, he could just distinguish a bat with a single wing and a newt with only one eye. The toad was missing an eye as well, but also his left front leg. Propped up with a sturdy stick, he began to tell the new arrival why the group were lacking various body parts.

'The fact is, my lad, she's been cooking bits of us on her show! We've listened to her as she smiles into the camera, telling her audience about the importance of using only fresh ingredients. Nice as pie she is then, but we never know which witch is which. One minute she's ripping limbs off and gouging eyes out with a throaty cackle, and the next she's droning on about coriander garnishes, whatever they are. Oh, and don't get me started on her take on 'Toad-in-the-Hole' from last week's show. I had a lucky escape there, and I'm trembling now just thinking about it!'

The bat managed to offer a semblance of comfort by shuffling around so that it's one wing covered most of the toad's back, the closest thing to a hug it could manage. The newt just stared into the semi-darkness, and baby frog felt a mixture of sympathy and horror.

'That's terrible! Can't we stop her?'

The newt shuddered with fear as she gave her answer.

'Well, it's not actually her who finds us and takes us to the kitchen. She gets her familiar, a black cat called Montmorency, to do that. On her command, he fetches the necessary 'ingredients' in advance of each show, and we suffer the consequences.'

The toad continued with a dire warning that struck fear into the little creature's heart.

'We are all in grave danger. Montmorency was prowling around the garden early this morning, so his mistress must be getting ready for her next programme. He hasn't discovered our little hideaway yet, but it's only a matter of time before he does.'

The diminutive frog puffed out his chest as best he could, youthful defiance coursing through his skinny body.

'Well I think this is terrible! Something should be done about it! It's outrageous that she thinks she can get away with....'

He never finished the sentence. Something black and furry pushed its way into the small space, scattering the fireflies and forcing everyone to move backwards in terror, apart from the unprepared youngster.

Montmorency withdrew his paw and grinned, whiskers taut as piano wire. One of his scythe-like claws had pierced the little one's skin and he watched as it struggled helplessly.

'How fortuitous! You happen to be top of Mistress's shopping list this week! My, she *will* be pleased, although it's a shame you're slightly damaged. As I recall, you're needed whole for the dessert course, something about being baked alive in sweet pastry to keep all the lovely juices in. Why, this could be the best episode of 'A Spell of Home Cooking' yet!'

Montmorency deftly used his teeth to lift the terrified frog from his paw and set off with tail held high towards the house. With his prey held fast in his mouth, he felt certain that he would receive interesting offcuts and tidbits during the next recording.

'How I *love* this job,' Montmorency mused to himself, before sauntering through the open patio doors and heading for the kitchen.

SKETCHPAD

'Damn it! Why didn't I just pull it out of the hedge, and what if it isn't there when I return home?'

These questions had turned over and over in Brian's mind all morning and now it was nearly lunchtime. He'd barely been able to concentrate on work after seeing the pencil portrait on his way to catch the train.

Brian Harris had left his small terraced house fifteen minutes late, so there was no way he could have caught the 08:22. Feeling stressed and trying to make up time, he'd turned the corner into Miller Street, flustered and in no mood for distractions. Yet there it was, partly obscured by the close-trimmed boundary, but undoubtedly a sketch of his face in profile. Confused and fascinated in equal measure, Brian briefly considered grabbing the sketchpad, thinking that he might study the image properly on the train, but concerns over being late took hold.

~~~~

Brian tried his best to stay calm as he neared the hedge on his way home and realised that he was muttering repeatedly to himself.

'Please let it be there, please let it be there.'

It was, so he grabbed the pad of paper in one quick movement and almost ran to his house. Although his stomach was rumbling, Brian ignored the need for food and rushed upstairs to his study. He placed the sketchpad on his desk and noticed a yellow pencil, secured in the spiral wiring along the top edge. The portrait's subject stared down at the image.

Now able to scrutinise the drawing more closely, Brian was amazed by the level of almost photographic detail. That small pimple near his left eyebrow, the slight kink in his nose – it was all there, but how *could* it be? He had never been asked to sit for anyone and, as far as he knew, no-one had been studying him on the train, or anywhere else, for that matter.

Brian's mind began to swim with questions. Who was the artist, and why was the pad in the hedge in the first place? Was it waiting for him to find it there? His eyes scanned every part of the sketch and its surrounding area, hoping to find a signature or other clue as to its creator, but there was no such mark. Brian pulled the pencil away from the metal binding. He noticed that it had clearly been reduced in length, presumably through sharpening, but was surprised to see the letters 'BH' near the rubber.

'Surely that should be 'HB' on a pencil? Hold on.... 'B' and 'H' are *my* initials!'

Unnerved by this possible connection, he placed the pencil on the desk and turned his attention to other illustrations in the sketch pad.

Brian soon realised that each drawing related directly to his life. There was a detailed image of his parents, although their faces were noticeably paler than their clothing. Perhaps, Brian thought, the ghostly features related to their passing over seven years ago. He missed them terribly and paused before turning to the next piece.

Oh, no! This was what Brian had been dreading, for his eyes fell upon a simple picture, executed in a child's hand. The figures were stick-like, with a name scrawled underneath each one – Mummy, Daddy,

Ben, Jenna and Josie. Five in the family group, yes, but three of them had been ripped out, leaving only broken outlines.

Brian's tears splashed onto the paper as he remembered the moment when the police officer told him that his wife, son and one of his twin daughters had been killed on the motorway. Trembling, he turned over to the next page to find an image of Josie, his only surviving child. She was pictured facing away from him, some of the pencil strokes so aggressive that they'd torn through into the next sheet.

How Brian wished he'd stayed in touch with Josie now. She had lived on her own in Bristol since graduating and there had been no contact between them for twelve years. Twelve years! He knew Josie still found it incredibly difficult to cope with the loss, but what about her dad? Couldn't they support each other?

Brian picked up the pencil bearing his initials. Rolling it between his fingers, he realised that it was life's sorrows that had worn it down to this point, but he saw a chance to stop it shortening as quickly in the years to come. Noticing that the sketch of Josie was the last entry, he determined to text her in the morning with a view to meeting up. It didn't matter where.

Brian slowly closed the sketchpad and looked around the room. He was filled with a bittersweet mixture of regret for the past and hope for the future. This was a strange amalgam, but one that demanded acknowledgement. It was then that a revelation crashed into Brian's thoughts, the instant clarity causing him to spring from his chair.

He was the artist! For over a decade, he had forced down the crushing pain of losing most of his family. The portraits, including those that had been ripped out, were manifestations of that all-consuming denial. Well, no more.

Brian picked up the sketchpad and hugged it tightly. As joy surged through his heart, he knew that every drawing that appeared from that moment would be of *happy* memories, starting with his meeting with Josie. Furthermore, there would be no need to use the pencil's eraser to rub out mistakes in the future, for Brian was determined to live life to the full. Things were going to change, and for the better.

MIRROR, MIRROR: 1

Two figures stand together in a dilapidated farmhouse, situated in the darkest part of the forest. There are two chipped plates on the dining table, licked clean of blood and bones.

'Don't look in the mirror!'

'Why not?'

'After what happened last time? Give me a break!'

'Break? Oh, very funny! I suppose now you're going to blame me for our seven years of bad luck!'

'Well, *yes*! It was *you* who decided to ignore basic Troll Lore and do the one thing you knew you shouldn't! Let's see now. When exactly was that?'

'You know very well it was Tuesday.'

'Hmm. It's Friday now, so that means we've got over 2,500 days of abject misery, soured milk, non-laying chickens and general upset to get through, and all because you just had to check if your lipstick was on straight!'

'Well, excuse me if I wanted to look beautiful for you! Don't you love me anymore?'

'Look.... I've been meaning to talk to you about that. Listen to me. Trolls are incredibly ugly, and we don't fall in love. Ever since you sat under the bridge last month and heard those humans above you, talking all lovey-dovey – YECH! – you've changed, and all because after eating them you decided to keep the female's make-up bag.'

'But she was so pretty! Not much meat on her, mind, but I learned so much about looking lovely and feelings and tenderness and.... well, everything!'

'That's as maybe, but who was it who swept up all the broken glass and still has the splinters to prove it? Me!'

'Oh, do stop complaining! Anyway, why have you put another mirror up, and why was there one there in the first place?'

'I don't know! I didn't write this fairy tale. Ask the author! Clearly, she didn't think this one through properly. I mean, how could I have hung either of them on the wall, if looking into them carries such dire consequences?'

'That *is* a good point. She's usually so reliable with our storylines, filling our lives with savage murders, unsuspecting victims and blood-soaked rituals. Remember that tale she wrote last year where we terrorised, slaughtered and ate a whole village in one night?'

'I certainly do. That was *lovely*. Hang on.... I think I know what's happened here.'

'Really?'

'Yes, I do. I reckon *she's* fallen in love!'

'Oh....'

'That's gross, if truth be told. I wasn't going to say anything, but I felt quite queasy when I had to talk to you about your beauty obsession earlier. It's clearly time to take control, so wipe that rouge off your tusks! Unless our lovesick creator makes us harbingers of pure evil and devourers of living flesh again, like we're *supposed* to be, well, it's all over!'

'Come on. Let's go and lurk under our favourite bridge and wait for unsuspecting fresh meat to walk across. You know, do what comes naturally.'

'That's more like it! I can almost hear the crunch of bones and taste the sweet, sweet marrow. Affairs of the heart, is it? She's welcome to all that! Just let me sink my rotten fangs into one that's still pumping. That's what'll keep *me* happy!'

Two figures stand together in the living room of a small house, situated in deepest suburbia. There are two empty plates on the dining table, licked clean of grass and leaves.

'Don't look in the mirror!'

'I completely forgot, Commander. If you wish it, I will self-evaporate immediately, putting an end to my stupidity.'

'That will not be necessary as we're not in view of the public here, but you must be more careful! You were told *several* times during training that humans can see our true selves in reflections! Repeat the mantra, to prove to me that you were listening.'

'DO NOT PASS THE MIRRORED GLASS. DO NOT PASS THE MIRRORED GLASS. DO NOT PASS THE MIRRORED GLASS. DO NOT PASS THE MIRRORED....'

'Very well. That's enough. The scouting mission is going extremely well, so nothing and *no-one* must be allowed to jeopardise it. In just a few more earth days, we can leave this pathetic rock and its pompous little monkeys behind as they parade around, destroying everything and killing each other. I can't wait to see their faces when the first harvester ships arrive. They'll assume that it's *them* we want to eat, never imagining for one of their seconds that we're a vegan race, able to strip their planet of every plant in moments.

'We've had to watch them stuffing their faces with bits of dead animal during our time here, and I for one will be glad to leave them to their sorry fate. They'll soon realise that they won't be able to survive for long without plants. Because we will take every blade of grass with us, they will have nothing with which to feed their doomed animals. Eventually their thoughts will turn to cannibalism and, because they're so stupid, they'll bring their race closer to extinction by their own hand.'

'But won't that mean we'll destroy *all* living things with the harvesting process, Commander? Some of the creatures here are rather beautiful.'

'Enough of such talk! Are you seriously telling me that the inhabitants of this planet are more important than ours? The nourishment from here will last us for several biospans, so there is no need or place for regret in this circumstance. I thought you understood that!'

The Commander looks at her subordinate questioningly, making the soldier feel uneasy, and with good reason.

'I've.... reconsidered my decision after this little conversation. Clearly you have misgivings about this whole project, even though it secures the long-term future of our race. Here, let me save you the trouble of self-evaporation.'

The Commander places her convincingly human hand on the soldier's forehead. He immediately disappears into the stale air, leaving only a few small green droplets on the swirl-patterned carpet. His superior smiles briefly and walks towards the door, satisfied that everything is on schedule.

MIRROR, MIRROR: 3

The setting is an odd landscape containing no sharp edges, with everything shaded in a light brown. It is populated by several figures, but only one is moving, dancing around and clapping his hands with glee.

'Don't look in the mirror!'

'Oh, it's too late for warnings because the process has already started, a process you know only too well.'

'This is terrible! I can't bear to see someone else going through it, and this one's only a child.'

'Exactly, so the transformation won't take long at all. Look! The boy has almost transferred already. As with yourself, once this is complete, the grains will start to spread upwards. They will change and claim him, so soon I'll have a new figure to place wherever I choose.'

'I curse you, Sandman! Someone somewhere will find a way to stop you!'

'Oh really? I distinctly remember telling you that my egg-timer shaped mirror is indestructible. There will always be people who find it oh-so-unusual and wish to hang it in their homes, so I will never run short of figures to populate my beautiful landscape.'

'What's beautiful about this? Everything's static and the same colour!'

Well *I* love it here and that's all that matters. I'm especially proud of the sea. Those sand waves took ages to curve and ripple like that, and the trees over there in the distance look very natural to *my* eyes.'

'You're acting like a god, Sandman, and you have no right to do so!'

'Silence! *You* are the one with no rights in my world. The sand has almost reached your shoulders, so it won't be long before you finally shut up!'

'That may be true but, while I can still talk, I'll continue to speak my mind. You're just a nasty, skinny coward, trapping innocent people just so that you can avoid being alone, and I despise every single grain that makes up this dreadful place!'

'But don't you see? You'll soon be completely made of sand yourself, so your pathetic outbursts mean nothing here. Surely even you must admire those massive sand sculptures of my head on the clifftop. A great likeness, don't you think?'

'Oh yes, I forgot to mention your insufferable vanity, Sandman! If I could, I'd topple them as a sign that you *will* be defeated one day!'

'But you can't, can you? Besides, you're also vain for looking in the mirror in the first place, so you have no right to condemn me, especially in my own kingdom. Now, if you will excuse me, I must welcome this new addition to my collection.'

The spindly figure skips across the sand to where the boy is standing, now fully relocated to this place of soft edges. The Sandman dances around him and cackles in victory, watching as the grains effortlessly begin the process of transforming the child's trainers.

MARK OF THE LION KING

We find ourselves on a cold, frosty mid-January morning deep in the London suburbs, where Julie lives with Jennifer, her mother, and six-year old daughter, Sophie. Granny is in the kitchen, trying to interest the youngster in healthy breakfast options. Julie had only one thing to say as she left for work twenty minutes ago.

'Good luck with that, Mum!'

For Julie has regularly found her resolve yielding to advertising pressure and pester power, a difficult combination to ignore. She recently considered buying boxes of so-called healthy breakfast bakes. She decided against these, however, after watching a television programme on the subject, during which it was stated that each one has more sugar than an average chocolate bar.

They need to leave for school in just under half an hour and Sophie has started to cry. She is just about to throw her spoon on the wooden floor when Jennifer has an idea. It sends her thoughts in a straight line back to her own childhood and a breakfast ritual that was hers and hers alone.

~~~~

A breakfast table in 1969. Matching crockery bearing a poppy design has been placed near a grey pottery teapot. An unopened jar of marmalade sits next to slightly burnt triangles of toast in the stainless-steel rack. A new box of malted cereal remains untouched, all because Jennifer Cooke, aged seven and a half, has taken a liking to soft-boiled eggs.

Is it because of the white bread soldiers that she enjoys dipping into the sunshine yellow yolk, or the pleasure she takes in slicing off the top with one sweep of the knife? Perhaps it is because she has her own blue and white striped egg cup. No, it is more than all of these put together, for Jennifer has found a new friend.

At first, her mother wondered why Jennifer was whispering close to the tablecloth every morning, but soon realised that she was addressing the lion on the side of the egg. She could see no harm in it, especially as her daughter was always smiling when she spoke to this pint-sized king of beasts.

As with most childhood fads and fancies, this one was replaced by another in a matter of weeks and soon forgotten. That is, until now.

~~~~

Jennifer wipes away Sophie's tears and offers a comforting smile. She takes a single egg from the egg-box, turns it so that the red lion is facing Sophie and starts to make soft roaring sounds. The child, puzzled at first, claps and smiles, then repeats Granny's noises as the lion comes closer.

'Say hello to The Lion King, Sophie! Look, he's even got a crown!'

Jennifer can see that her granddaughter is intrigued, so she takes it a stage further.

'He's got his own army of soldiers *and* he tastes delicious! Would you like to have him for breakfast?'
'YES! YES!'

She gives the egg to Sophie, who kisses the little lion before passing it back to her grandmother. As she sets a pan of water to boil, Jennifer warmly realises that history repeating itself can sometimes be a *good* thing. She quietly asks herself one question:

'Now, where did I put that blue and white egg cup?'

THE BOATMAN

Jake had always loved the river, a love that started when his father Stephen made him a small blue boat for his sixth birthday. It was nothing fancy, simply painted and with only rudimentary sails, but it meant everything to the boy. He imagined a miniature version of himself sailing the oceans in the little craft, navigating stormy seas and enjoying calmer waters.

The river flows on, away from the source....

It was inevitable that Jake would follow in his father's footsteps. Stephen owned a large boatyard and his son always enjoyed spending time there. During his teens, Jake would often hurry down to the yard after school and help to clean the boats or generally keep the place tidy. He went on to study boatbuilding in Lowestoft, and his tutors found him to be an excellent student with a strong desire to succeed.

The river flows on, deeper and wider....

After graduation, Jake returned home to work in the family business. This decision filled his father's heart with pride, and the pair worked well together for over a decade. Jake inherited the business at the age of thirty-five when Stephen passed away, and the young man devoted himself wholeheartedly to maintaining his father's standards, both in quality of design and hard work.

The river flows on, running stronger and faster....

But then came Janie. He had never met anyone like her before. There had been girlfriends, yes, but none had possessed that spark, that lightness of spirit and he was captivated from the very first smile. She encouraged Jake to think big and expand the business. Never a natural risk taker, he bit his lip and followed her lead, conceding eventually that she had been right all along.

The river flows on, dappled with sunlight....

Life felt wonderful for Jake and Janie. Even their names dovetailed like a perfect deck beam joint on one of his boats and he couldn't imagine life without her. Within four years, however, wide cracks had appeared in their love, threatening to split the hull and sink their relationship.

The river flows on, via rapids and rocks....

Jake was heartbroken when Janie left him, but he threw himself into his work and found solace there. Even though equilibrium gradually returned, the boatman vowed that he would never let anyone get close enough to hurt him again.

The river flows on, calm but a little colder....

The business became highly successful and eventually spread to three boatyards, making Jake a very wealthy man. If anything, his love of boatbuilding increased over the years. As time rolled on, however, tiredness started to seep into his bones like a leaky vessel and he reluctantly considered retirement.

The river flows on, slowly to the sea....

Which is why we now find Jake on a cruise ship in the Adriatic, after his 'second in command' told him he ought to take a well-earned holiday.

~~~~

The boat is listing dramatically on the port side, having earlier struck a rock. Ten minutes ago, Jake fell over and hit his head hard on a table. Blood is now streaming from the wound, staining the expensive carpet. With consciousness ebbing away but determined, the boatman manages to reach his suitcase. He fumbles with the clasps, opens it and takes out what is, in that moment, the most important thing in the world to him.

As the screams outside his cabin continue, Jake clutches the small blue boat to his blood-spattered shirt, smiles and closes his eyes for the last time.

BULGING CURTAINS

In a quiet cul-de-sac, a married couple, Ella and Fenton, are about to have a familiar argument, unaware that a third individual is listening.

'Well, where are they, Ella?'

'Where are what? You'll have to be more specific than *that*!'

'The box of iced buns I bought at the bakery this lunchtime. I put them on the low table over there when I came in.'

'Oh, here we go!'

'What do you mean?'

'You're assuming I ate them all when you went to make the coffees. Typical! Why can't you just come out and say it, Fenton? You think I'm fat and disgusting and I can't control my food cravings!'

'Well you could.... lose a few pounds, yes....'

'Thanks for that!'

'Hey, I'm not accusing you, Ella, but *someone* must have eaten them and eaten them very quickly, because the box looks like it's been trampled on.'

'And you think it's me because I'm the only person in here. Look at me, Fenton! Do you see any crumbs on my clothes or icing around my lips? There would surely be some if I'd stuffed my face that fast!'

'I.... I don't want to talk about it.'

'Exactly! You never do, and that's the problem around here!'

A silence ensues, crackling with tension. Then....

'Ooh! Whatever was that?'

'What?'

'That trumpeting sound just now.'

'I didn't hear anything.'

'Was it.... you, Fenton?'

'Oh, so now it's *my* turn, is it? You know how hard it is for me to discuss my.... condition. I thought you understood, and you know it can't be helped.'

'Can't it? We never discuss it, so why are you so sure that no help is available?'

'I.... I....'

'I know, I know! You don't want to talk about it! Let's just leave it then like we always do. No discussion, no debate, no solution and no compromise. I'll go and make a start on the tea, but I have to tell you that I can't take this much longer!'

Ella storms into the kitchen in a rage and slams the door. Fenton sees a small blizzard of crumbs on the carpet beneath the window, along with a few shards of white icing. He is utterly exhausted after a difficult day at the office, so only vaguely notices the large bulge behind the floor-length, emerald green curtains.

Fenton sits down in his favourite armchair to read the evening paper. Trying to ignore the angry clattering of pans and utensils emanating from the kitchen, he finds an advertisement on page thirty-eight that sets his curiosity aflame:

'ARE YOU HAVING TROUBLE COMMUNICATING WITH YOUR PARTNER? DO YOU FIND IT HARD TO TALK ABOUT EMBARRASSING, PERSONAL SUBJECTS WITH YOUR LOVED ONE? WELL DON'T JUST SUFFER IN SILENCE! CONTACT 'MAMMOTH MATRIMONIAL SOLUTIONS' INSTEAD, BECAUSE WE'RE HERE TO HELP. CALL THIS NUMBER TODAY!'

Fenton carefully tears the advert from the newspaper, places it in his trouser pocket and proudly declares his intention:

'I can't take this much longer either, Ella, so I'm going to ring 'Mammoth Matrimonial Solutions' in the morning. It's only the first step, my love, but we have to sort this out, once and for all.'

He smiles to himself, happy with the decision to take the path of openness, free of accusation and blame. Behind the long, pleated curtains, a large shape starts to diminish, gradually becoming insignificant. Eventually it shrinks to the same size as the crumbs and icing, nestling on top of the grey shag pile.

REVENGE

Where have they all gone? Why have they left him alone? Confusion is a new sensation for him, and he doesn't know how to react. He has been part of a group, eating and sleeping together for as long as he can remember.

He had left the cave when the light was strong, to forage for plants and berries. A risky activity to undertake alone, yes, but he always enjoys the sounds of nature all around him whenever he ventures outside. This foray was unsuccessful, however, so now he stands near the entrance looking in at the fire, set in the cave's centre.

He tentatively steps forward in the unexpected silence and scratches his head, dislodging several fleas in the process. He drops to his knees in the dirt and stares deep into the dancing flames. He knows that he will be safe from attack whilst the fire burns brightly but, when it dies down, beasts of the night might enter the cave and find him there, a trapped meal of surrendering flesh and warm blood.

He lifts his eyes and looks around the cave, studying his work. The red and black images he creates from charcoal and oxides have given him an important role, for his paintings hold within them the spirits of those animals his brothers have killed, as well as the bravery displayed on every hunt. He never goes with them nor wants to and is simply happy to hold his special place within the family. The one who captures the essence of the beasts, the one who tells the stories of victory on the rough stone surface. So, if he and his pictures are of such value, why have they all left him there to fend for himself?

He hears a wolf howl in the dusk beyond the cave and feels a shudder, thinking of the night to come. Realising that the animal is quite close to the entrance, he stays as still as possible, careful not to make a sound. Staring down at the sandy floor, he vaguely notices an odd grey dust on top of the usual fine grains, but the next lupine cry from outside demands his attention. This one was somewhat quieter, which tells him that the creature has already slunk past in the spreading shadows. Relieved but weary, he lies down on the sand and closes his eyes to sleep as the fire continues to crackle and spit.

He wakes to animal grunts and howls, but they appear to be coming from *inside* the cave. He leaps up, startled and afraid, but can see no threatening intruder in the small space. Whilst he slept the flames diminished, taking their warmth with them, and now a cold, primal fear stabs at his heart. In the growing gloom, he strains to look at his paintings and notices that some changes have taken place, in that all the figures of men he created, stick-like with spears raised to strike, have disappeared. When he painted his images, he made sure that all his brothers were celebrated there, but now there are none. As he stares at the creatures, a further transformation occurs.

Each animal outline begins to tremble and move. Legs, hooves and antlers lift and lower again, then heads turn to face him. Eyes emerge, mere black dots of charcoal, but each pair burns with pure hatred, hatred for these bipedal butchers who have slaughtered to satisfy their endless need for fresh meat.

The stag, imposing even in this simplified form, throws its head back and emits a mighty bellow. Every other painted beast joins in, and the booming sound echoes around the cave. Terrified and trembling, he dissolves into a fine grey dust, much as his siblings had done. The animals whose spirits he successfully harnessed have avenged their fallen brothers and sisters at last.

The cave falls silent once more as each image returns to profile, static and newly victorious. The curious wolf returns later, and this time enters the now empty space. The creature circles and sniffs at the dying embers, leaving its paw prints in the powdery grey.

COMPOUND EYES

Meet Margaret. She's always raising the left side of her living room nets to see what's going on in Poplar Road. Since Roland died nearly five years ago, Margaret has spent a large part of each day sitting in the faded green armchair near the window, waiting for something, *anything* to happen outside, within sight of No. 28.

Roland used to complain to Margaret about her nosiness, a milder behaviour trait in those days. He would hear her tutting disapprovingly and lower his broadsheet newspaper, enough to see his wife craning her neck like some curious stork, trying to observe some change or other. He would loudly clear his throat to indicate his annoyance, but Margaret always ignored him. She was far too interested in who was walking past, especially if they were not people she recognised. In those circumstances, she would rush to the front door, hurry down the path and lean over the gate to get a better look before they disappeared. Margaret used to run back into the house if she spotted which gate had been opened, and eagerly tell Roland the 'breaking news'. He would merely raise his newspaper again, a useful printed barrier to keep her nonsense at bay.

Over the past few days, however, something *very* unusual has been happening at No. 31, directly opposite Margaret's house. Each evening, at precisely 8.00 p.m., three men dressed in black overcoats arrive. Their collars are turned up and they wear trilbies, looking for all the world like gangsters from the 1930s. Margaret is annoyed that she cannot see their faces, but far more intriguing are the bulging black refuse sacks carried by these obviously shady characters.

Oh, and then there is the 'special' knock on the door. Three sharp raps followed by four in quick succession, with a final single strike, louder than the others. Margaret, besides herself with curiosity, has watched as the door slowly opens each time. The strangers always look around to check that they are not being observed (on the contrary they are, and by one of the best), then hurry inside for their clandestine meeting.

~~~~

The mantel clock has just struck the quarter hour after eight on this, the fifth evening. Margaret paces up and down, plagued by those key questions we all learnt in childhood - Who? What? Why? When? How? – but, more specifically:

'Who are these men? What is in those bags? Why 8.00 p.m. on the dot?'

The last two queries relate to her sheer frustration:

'When can I find out more? How can I get in there without being seen?'

Margaret's attention is drawn to movement at the top of the net curtains. She watches as the small creature rubs its front legs together then flies around the room, before landing again on the semi-transparent fabric. Poplar Road's nosey parker shudders as a recent image resurfaces, an image of a child's arm poking out of one of the stranger's bags. Did she *really* see that a few minutes ago? Margaret gives voice to an odd thought as the insect jerkily climbs the curtain:

'I'd love to be one of you, over there at No. 31....'

~ ~ ~ ~

Margaret, aware that her field of vision is suddenly much wider, is surprised to find that she now has six legs and is standing upside down on the ceiling. Below her she sees three men wearing overcoats and hats, all talking to a woman in a front room very much like her own. Margaret's antennae pick up the conversation, but the words are muffled, so she instinctively launches off the ceiling. Her first attempt at flight is understandably clumsy but, after a couple of circuits, she gains in confidence and lands on the rim of a large, ivory-white lampshade.

Feeling an urgent need to groom, Margaret rubs her forelegs over her eyes to dislodge particles of dirt, then concentrates on what is being said nearby. What she hears makes her wish that she had stayed on the ceiling.

'I bet the nosey old bat opposite is wetting herself, desperate to find out what's been going on over the road!'

'Serves her right. We've all seen her nets trembling as we've walked past No. 28. I've often wanted to stick two fingers up to her window, but I wouldn't give her the satisfaction that she's been noticed. This was such a great idea, Connie!'

'Thanks, but it was *your* masterstroke to have that doll's arm poking out of the bag this evening. She'll be beside herself now!'

'A bit cruel, I suppose, but I just couldn't resist!'

Everyone laughs and one of the 'gangsters' takes off his trilby. The other men follow suit, and Margaret instantly recognises their faces. Brian, Patrick and Martin live in Poplar Road as well! Connie clearly cooked this up with her neighbours to mock her, never

74

imagining for a moment that their object of ridicule would find out about it. Angry now, Margaret defecates on the lampshade's edge then flies over the pranksters' heads in a wide circle, landing on the sideboard. The conversation continues.

'I passed her in the street yesterday afternoon. It was all I could do to keep a straight face.'

'I'm surprised she didn't stop you and ask if you knew anything about the 'peculiar goings on' at No. 31!'

'Thank goodness she didn't, Brian, because that would have set me off!'

Laughter breaks out again and Margaret's little body trembles with rage. Her curiosity has been satisfied, yes, but at such a humiliating cost. She is just about to take off again when....

A sudden burst of incredible pain. Body parts rupturing, flattening, collapsing. Crushed organs and damaged wings on printed paper. End.

Patrick puts Connie's newspaper back on her coffee table, then addresses his co-conspirators.

'I think we should make tomorrow's meeting the last one. She might start to lose interest if there are too many of them.'

'I agree. Also, if the visits suddenly end, she'll be left wondering *why* they've stopped. Another level of torment!'

'Great. OK, Connie, we'll be off now.'

'Thanks, all of you. I just love the thought of her stewing behind those nets and wondering why she never sees anybody leave!'

Hugs and knowing smiles are exchanged before Brian, Patrick and Martin pick up their black sacks.

Connie leads them through the kitchen, opens the back door and ushers them outside. The 'gangsters' wave as they walk down the shadowed garden to the gate, each one already looking forward to tomorrow evening.

Connie grins as she locks up for the night. Back in the living room, she notices the splattered fly on the newspaper, squashed earlier by Patrick. Wearing an expression of distaste, she gingerly carries the stained tabloid into the kitchen, steps on the pedal of her bin and drops it inside.

ACCLAIM

'.... and the award goes to.... Troy Carter!'

'Well, thank you so much! It's an honour just to be here at the Annual Annoyance Awards, but to be presented with something.... that's amazing.

'I guess I'd like to thank three groups of people who helped me to win 'MOST IRRITATING USE OF A MOBILE DEVICE IN PUBLIC' - although none of them would want my gratitude, let's face it!

'Firstly, to those people who walked into me when I stopped for no reason in the street. The angry looks they gave me. Priceless!

'Up next are the individuals who tutted and moaned about me, complaining that 'everyone is looking down nowadays, living their lives through little screens'. Those guys probably thought I wasn't listening. Well, I was. I heard everything they said, and they unwittingly inspired me to become even more annoying, which leads me on to the third group.

'I enjoyed these the most. I'd stop someone and ask for directions to, say, a coffee shop, whilst staring down at my phone with my headphones on. It would be all I could do to stop laughing when they'd start to shout information at me before walking off in sheer frustration.

'I'd like to acknowledge two of the other winners here this evening. I guess we three must have offended hundreds between us!

'Trudi Long. What can I say? You thoroughly deserve 'LOUDEST CONVERSATION ON PUBLIC TRANSPORT'. I've seen, or rather, heard you in full flow myself, and you were completely oblivious to the other passengers' anger. Magnificent, Trudi.

'As for Cindy Sharp. Who else could win 'FASTEST AT PLUGGING IN AND UTILISING DEVICES ON A TRAIN'? Twelve seconds to start charging a mobile phone and set up a laptop on one of those little fold-down tables? Great work, Cindy, great work.

'I'd also like to mention the judging panel who discreetly viewed my efforts over the past few months. I was amazed when one of them approached me – in Trafalgar Square, as I recall – to tell me that I'd been nominated.

'Finally, I urge you all to look at the word displayed on the screen behind me. I'd arranged for it to be flashed up there if I won tonight, but it's also for Trudi and Cindy. After all, it's the reason we're gathered here this evening, so shout it out as loudly as you can, three times for maximum impact.

So – on three, then.... one, two, three....

IRRITATION! IRRITATION! IRRI....

Oh, please excuse me. I must just take this call. It's bound to be important....'

THE ARGUMENT

They glare at each other. Lars is seated at the bow with Marielle at the stern, neither attempting to hide the hatred in their eyes. If truth be told, both are racked with fear at the rise and fall of the waves, each swell seemingly greater than the last. With no oars or rudder to steer their small vessel, they are completely at the mercy of the argument's duration and intensity.

They can't remember how this one began but, like so many before, it probably blew up from something vague or insignificant. The waves were little more than ripples in their emotional sea when it started, lightly crested with foam and untroubling, but now the peaks and troughs are dramatic in the extreme. Lars grips the sides of the boat, determined not to show Marielle how scared he has become, but notices that his other, equally bitter half is holding on just as tightly and is also struggling to maintain a semblance of calm.

Two large fish are lifted by the tumultuous waters and thrown over the sides of the small wooden craft. They flop at the feet of the warring couple, thrashing wildly. Lars and Marielle, temporarily distracted, look down at them and are disturbed to find that these creatures bear their own faces, twisted in contempt. The fish frantically gasp for air but, before they breathe their last, manage to sink needle sharp teeth into human flesh. Lars and Marielle hadn't even noticed that their feet are bare and now, as they scream with pain, realise that these strange beings are manifestations of their loathing for each other, nothing more, nothing less.

Lars and Marielle had averted their eyes when the fish appeared, but now resume their face off in smouldering silence. There is no need to speak, for now the wind begins to communicate with them, frenziedly whipping and whirling through the dark grey clouds. It whistles past their ears, whispering fresh accusations and echoes of unresolved arguments as it passes. This intervention only serves to increase Lars's animosity towards Marielle and vice versa, making the waves even more tempestuous.

Still staring at Lars, Marielle thinks she glimpses land in her peripheral vision. She turns her head slightly and finds that her eyes were not deceiving her. Lars wonders why she has broken her icy stare and is further confused when she smiles at him, reaches forward and takes his hands in hers.

'Look, all this fighting is exhausting, and I've really had enough. Besides, we weren't always like this, remember? Turn around, Lars, and tell me what you see.'

She releases her gentle grip and points towards what is, in fact, quite a large island. Disarmed but curious, Lars turns and is surprised by what meets his gaze. He sees a sunlit shoreline with swaying palms behind, and notices that the dark grey clouds above them are bleeding into a deep cobalt, as if an experienced watercolourist is painting the sky.

That shade reminds Lars of happier times, when he and Marielle would just relax together, either sitting on a beach or in a meadow, beneath the cloudless blue. He smiles at Marielle, then tentatively moves towards the stern and takes her in his arms. Neither is particularly surprised to find that the angry waters have lost their fury, or that their little boat has set sail for those golden sands, supported on gentle waves of optimism and reconciliation.

EAT YOUR GREENS OR....

Lunchtime in a school canteen, 1964. Grey-brown slices of meat, cabbage boiled into submission, bullet hard sprouts and lumpy mash, the whole smothered in barely warm, congealing gravy.

Richard, four years old and unhappy, stared down at the plate before him, desperately wishing he could be at home. His first day at primary school began badly enough, watching his mother walk away with a wave and a nervous smile on her face. His tearful howls had nearly drowned out the hand bell, rung by a teacher to call the children indoors for registration and the start of the first lesson, but this was far worse.

He shut his eyes as tightly as he could and tried to will the laden plate away but, when he opened them again, he saw that it had stubbornly remained in place. Richard looked around the table, to find that most of his fellow pupils had already moved on to their desserts, a choice of either gluey semolina with a blotch of red jam or treacle sponge and canary yellow custard. These brightly coloured dishes appeared much more appealing than Richard's plate of drab, barely touched food.

After pushing two sprouts around a little to appear interested, he looked up and saw one of the dinner ladies chatting with Mr. Jarvis, the teacher on lunch duty that day. Richard was clearly the focus of their conversation.

The boy averted his gaze and stared at the plate again, but soon became aware of an imposing figure standing next to him.

'What's your name?'
'Richard Burrows, Sir.'

'Well, Richard Burrows, you're coming with me. Bring your plate and cutlery with you.'

Disconsolate, Richard stood up and did as he was told. A boy on the next table, having stirred his jam and semolina together, loaded his spoon with some of the pink goo, ready to flick in Richard's direction. A withering look from Mr. Jarvis, however, rapidly changed his mind and the spoon was lowered in defeat.

Richard followed the teacher into a large classroom. The plate appeared to be getting heavier and he longed to put it down, so he was relieved when Mr. Jarvis told him to sit.

'Now, young Burrows. You're going to stay there until you've eaten everything. There are plenty of starving people around the world who would be more than grateful for this wonderful meal. I want you to think about that for a moment. I must get back to the canteen but, when I return, I want to see an empty plate. Otherwise, you'll be in trouble.'

Mr. Jarvis left the room, closing the door firmly behind him. Richard was glad to be left alone and forced himself to look down at the plate. Amazingly, the food looked even more unappetising than before. He pushed it away, rested his arms on the desk and cradled his head. Heaving sobs racked his body and he scrunched his eyes tightly, longing for *someone* or *something* to help.

~~~~

Richard heard footsteps approaching the door. The leader of his own personal gang, newly created and hideous, was hiding behind a large cupboard. It put a bony green finger to its rubbery lips and the boy immediately understood what it meant. Richard could hardly wait for the fun to begin.

Mr. Jarvis entered the room and looked at the plate of food. He shook his head as he approached Richard, annoyed that the child was smirking.

'There's nothing funny about this, Burrows. I'll be speaking to the headmaster about this, mark my words.'

'But look, Sir. The *sprouts* have gone.'

'Alright. I'll give you that, but it's really not the....'

A sinewy arm wrapped around Mr. Jarvis's throat. Forcibly dragged to the front of the class, he was only able to gurgle a protest before being released. He turned to face his aggressor and could hardly believe what he saw.

It was a Brussels sprout, six feet tall, brassica green and heavily fanged. It stood drooling on legs that appeared far too spindly to support its weight. It breathed over Mr. Jarvis, the foul, fetid stink of rotten vegetation making him choke and retch. He started to tremble as five slightly smaller sprouts left their hiding places behind the middle desks and joined their leader.

The frenzied attack started immediately. Two of the sprouts pushed Mr. Jarvis to the floor, after which all six set upon him, deranged with hunger. Richard stood up and laughed as he hurled handfuls of mashed potato and soggy cabbage at the sprouts' hapless victim.

They ate everything and even licked the floor clean, leaving no trace of 'lunch'. With blood drying on their fangs, the grisly sextet courteously bowed low to Richard before springing towards the window. The largest smashed the glass with both fists, let out a high-pitched squeal and leapt outside. The others followed and they all ran away across the playing fields and into the woods beyond.

Young Mr. Burrows sat down and smiled. He heard the bell for afternoon lessons and carried his plate to the broken window. He threw it onto the tarmac and casually left the classroom without a care in the world.

BACCHUS IS BACK!

In a ground floor flat on Temperance Street in October, an argument is brewing, or perhaps that should be fermenting.

'Well *I'm* not going up there again, Norma!'

'Somebody has to, George! That weird stain on the ceiling is spreading wider by the minute!'

'Look, I'm sure it will just stop eventually. It might even start to dry out.'

'Dry out? You're pathetic!'

'I'm just no good with confrontation, that's all.'

'I bet you didn't even knock yesterday, did you? Did you, George?'

'I knocked robustly on the door, I promise you, Norma. Three times, to be precise.'

'And what good did your robust knocking achieve? Precisely nothing!'

'As I explained when I came back downstairs, it's no surprise that no-one answered the door because they were enjoying themselves so much.'

'Well, I can't stand another sleepless night, George, and it's not as if they've stopped during the day. I mean, whatever are they *doing* up there?'

'I'm sure they're just having a nice little party to celebrate moving in, Norma.'

'A nice little party? With all those women shrieking and laughing all the time, and those animal grunts and snarls in the background? Oh, and that endless flute music!'

'I have to say I rather like it, Norma.'

'Perhaps it wouldn't be so bad if they weren't clomping up and down dancing to it! It sounds like a herd of wild animals up there!'

'I'm sure it will all calm down once they get tired.'

'Calm down? I'll show them calm down! I'm going up there right now!'

With that, Norma leaves the apartment and storms up the stairs in a rage. She bangs so hard on the door that her hand hurts, but she is determined to challenge the new neighbours.

The sounds of merrymaking suddenly cease, including the flute. The door opens a crack and a mischievous eye meets Norma's angry stare.

'Now, look here!'
'Can I help you, Madam?'
'I.... I....'

The door is opened half-way and the flautist strikes up again. Norma cranes her neck to see what is happening inside.

She sees naked women and strange, horned creatures offering them wine and much more besides. There are vines twisting and swaying to the music and bunches of plump grapes on every surface. Norma, rapt with curiosity, turns her attention to the figure in the doorway.

He is only young and the boyish glint in his eyes utterly entrances her. His tousled curly hair is topped by a crown of vines, leaves and grapes. He flashes her a smile of perfect white teeth and offers an invitation.

'Why don't you step inside for a moment and sup with us? We only have the very finest wines here. I should know, for I've travelled the world and helped to make them!'
'I shouldn't, really. Besides, I came up here to complain about the....'
'Ssssh! Don't worry about that now. Have a little drink with me and my.... friends.'

As if to encourage her in, a vine wraps itself around her shoulders and gently pushes her forwards. Once inside the room, one of the satyrs pours Norma what is to be the first of many glasses of wine. The horned sommelier licks his lips as she takes her first sip, then throws his head back and laughs.

The crowned host stands beside her. He smiles as a vine twists round the buttons on her cardigan and tears them from the fabric. By the second refill, all Norma's clothing has fallen away, and she can't stop giggling. In a haze, she looks around the room and sees a large wooden vat in the corner. It is full of grapes, and naked women are happily squishing them between their toes, laughing as they trample. The juice slurps and slops over the edges, a reddish-purple puddle spreading across the floorboards.

'Ah! That explains the stain on the ceiling, but much more worrying is that my glass appears to be empty!'
'That will *never* do, Madam. Allow me.'

As the chief reveller pours the wine, Norma becomes serious for a moment.

'You haven't asked me my name and I don't know yours.'
'Oh, such things don't matter here. Drink up!'

Norma notices activity near the vat. A pig is being led to a low table by two satyrs. Waiting there with a long knife is a third.

'What's happening over there?'
'Such beasts must be sacrificed for they are harmful to the grape harvest, the product of which you are now thoroughly enjoying.'
'Oh, that's alright then!'

Norma starts to giggle again, at which her host arches an eyebrow.

'Don't you.... need to be getting back?'
'Not really. I'll.... stay a little longer if that's alright....'
'Certainly, Madam. Make yourself at home.'

One of the vines silently pushes the door closed, sealing Norma in.

~ ~ ~ ~

Downstairs, George mumbles to himself, assessing the situation.

'Norma's taking her time up there and she only managed to get them to stop the noise for a few moments. I'm sure she'll come back soon with her tail between her legs, admitting she was wrong to make such a fuss.'

But she never does. As George sits ruminating with the stain spreading wider above him, a droplet falls onto his newspaper. The colour has changed to more of a purplish-brown, and when a drop lands on his forehead, he presses a finger to it and then touches his tongue.

'That's odd. It tastes of grapes, but there's something else, something metallic.'

When George realises that the extra element is blood, he looks up at the ceiling, certain that he can hear Norma's distinctive high laugh, piercing through the cacophony upstairs.

THE MISCHIEF SEED

Terry first noticed that something wasn't quite right when he boarded the steps of the aeroplane. One of the stewardesses showed genuine concern and asked if he needed assistance.

'No, I'll be fine, thank you. It's just a cough. I'm sure it will pass.'

But it didn't. It grew more persistent by the time he reached his middle seat, only ceasing after he gulped down the glass of water provided by another member of the flight crew. Relieved, Terry fastened his seat belt and watched his fellow passengers as they struggled to put their luggage in the overhead lockers.

It was then that the urge to giggle started to bubble up inside him. A childish smirk spread across Terry's face as a decidedly grumpy woman took the seat to his left. She looked at him with utter contempt, which only made him want to laugh even more.

For a fleeting moment, he considered kissing her full on the lips then blowing her a loud raspberry. What was happening to him? Terry knew that both actions were completely unacceptable, and that to follow either would probably get him thrown off the flight. Besides, he was a respectable businessman and never did anything that could be considered irrational. As he struggled to suppress this infantile urge, he recalled that Pamela had cited his 'lack of fun' as one of the reasons for their divorce.

'Still, she did bloody well out of the settlement! Getting on for half a million. Not bad, eh?'

Terry nudged the woman as he posed the question, at which she flashed him a look even more severe than the first.

That was it. Peals of laughter burst forth from him until he became red-faced and almost breathless. She summoned a stewardess and whispered her request to be moved to another seat, but she was informed that this wouldn't be possible as the flight was fully booked. Terry's guffaws gradually reduced to a few chuckles, however, after the flight attendant spoke to him with a firm politeness. Suitably admonished, he turned his attention to the man in the window seat.

'I want to sit there.'

'Excuse me?'

'*I* want to sit there.'

'Well perhaps you should have thought about that when you booked.'

Terry looked at the man for a moment, before tears welled up in his 56-year-old eyes. He wanted to stand to emphasise his resentment, but found it difficult to unfasten his seat belt, even though he was an experienced traveller. He managed to release it eventually and stood up. Terry towered over the seated figure, who was now rather nervous.

'I WANT THE WINDOW SEAT! I WANT THE WINDOW SEAT NOW!'

'Well, you can't have it!'

'NOW! NOW! NOW!'

The stewardess who had originally greeted Terry glided swiftly down the aisle to calm the situation, privately reflecting on his childish behaviour.

'Sir, I wonder if you'd mind letting this.... gentleman have the window seat. We'll be taking off shortly, and your assistance would calm the situation considerably.'

'But I paid to sit here! I don't see why I....'

'Please, Sir?'

'Oh, very well, but I'll be making a complaint, don't you worry!'

The men swapped places and fastened their seat belts again, and Terry peered out of the window in awe at the assorted aircraft on the tarmac.

'Big planes! Big, big planes *everywhere!*'

The adult Terry heard himself whispering these juvenile words, gurgling with pleasure as he did so. Something had changed inside him, and he became aware of a strange fizzing sensation in his stomach. He pondered that peculiar cough, as his childish counterpart enjoyed flipping the small tray table up and down as loudly as possible. Had the irritation in his throat been caused by a foreign body, perhaps a seed or a spore, or had he eaten something dodgy earlier? That tuna and sweetcorn sandwich at the airport had tasted fine but, whatever the reason, grown-up Terry was finding it increasingly difficult to maintain a grip on the situation, especially during take-off:

'WHEEEEEEEEEEEEEEEEEEEEEEEEE!'

The flight took an hour and a half, but for those sitting nearby it seemed to last at least twice as long. Terry was the only passenger enjoying himself, flicking bits of biscuit at the cabin crew, drawing obscene pictures on the safety information card or making rude noises as people returned to their seats after visiting the toilet.

The effects of the mischief seed started to wear off when the plane landed, however, and had diminished considerably by the time he reached the baggage carousel. The weakened but still playful version of Terry longed to climb onto the conveyor belt and ride the suitcases like a rodeo cowboy, but the adult form was steadily regaining control of both body and mind.

As he left the 'Arrivals' hall, Terry lazily scanned the printed names, held up to attract the attention of certain passengers - 'JOHNSON', 'MIKE WEBB', 'RUTH COLLINS' - but there was one sign that stopped him dead in his tracks. It read 'TERRY WARD' and ended with a question mark. He looked at the smiling boy holding the card and recognised that the child was the spitting image of *him* in his early teens. Terry cleared his throat, tightened his grip on the extended handle of his suitcase and marched purposefully past the younger version of himself.

Under his breath, Terry acknowledged that the heady days of youth were long gone. He sighed heavily as he walked through the sliding doors and on towards the taxi rank. Dimly remembering his recent behaviour, he suddenly understood why his fellow passengers had given him such strange looks as they left the plane, but then a disturbing thought entered his mind as he opened the cab door. What if the younger Terry were to appear again in the future, perhaps looking up at the window during an important business meeting, or standing at the back of a conference centre?

The troubled businessman scanned the pavement with nervous eyes as the taxi set off. An end to childhood? Maybe not, after all....

IT'S GRIMM OUT THERE

In an alternative fairy tale universe in the depths of winter, it's time for seven sleepyheads to get up.

'Come on, you lot! If you're not down the mine at the start of shift there'll be trouble!'

One diminutive figure pulls the duvet over his head, hoping to steal a few more minutes. Unfortunately for him, Mistress Jet Black knows this tactic only too well.

'Don't try that one again, Sloth! You've got work to do like all the others!'

She whips the covers off in one movement and Sloth stretches and yawns before grudgingly leaving his beloved bed. Mistress Jet Black turns her attention to the kitchen, where another familiar pattern of behaviour has already started.

'Gluttony! You've had quite enough already, so stop stealing from Greed's bowl. You know how angry it makes him!'
'Oh, don't worry, Mistress, because I got up in the night and ate a whole chocolate cake, a tray of muffins and.... Gluttony's whole packed lunch for today!'
''Why, Greed, you little....'
'That's enough, you two! Far be it from me as Empress of this evil realm to get all moralistic and balanced in my opinions, but it looks fair from where *I'm* standing. As for *you*, Lust, I've got a pretty good idea what you're doing under the table, so put it away and eat your breakfast.'

Mistress Jet Black knows where *one* of the seven has gone, so she stands outside the locked bathroom door and raps hard on it with a black-gloved fist.

'I know you're in there, Pride! If you don't stop preening in front of that mirror – and you *know* how much I detest mirrors - I'll break this door down. You've got five minutes!'

'Alright! Keep your crown on!'

Mistress Jet Black returns to the kitchen, only to find Gluttony and Greed scowling at each other, and Sloth with his head down in his bowl of porridge. She briskly claps her hands together, before addressing the six who are seated there.

'It's the same every morning! Why can't you be like Envy and Wrath? They *love* their work underground, digging out nuggets of hatred to hurl into the world of humans. Besides, I've got a whole tray of rosy red apples to inject with poison this morning, so clear off, the lot of you. NOW!'

Greed and Gluttony lift Sloth's head out of the large bowl and eagerly lick him clean of porridge. Pride reluctantly emerges from the bathroom, still checking his neat, white beard in a pocket mirror, until Mistress Jet Black snatches it out of his hand. He joins the others as they prepare to leave, finally ready to head out into the snow-white landscape.

REVERSE PSYCHOLOGY

He finds it on the foyer's wiry doormat on the morning of April 15th, the day after his birthday. It comes as an extra surprise, and not a welcome one.

The split had been acrimonious, but Louise and James knew that it was inevitable. During their relationship, there were times when they would barely acknowledge each other's presence. These periods often lasted for weeks, during which they wouldn't even share meals or watch television together. On the rare occasions when they *did* find themselves in the same space, bitter arguments would flare in a matter of minutes, after which they would retreat to lick their emotional wounds in separate rooms.

Since that July evening when Louise stormed out of the apartment with two suitcases, there had been no contact between them, apart from a few matter-of-fact text messages, heartless and cold. His love for Louise had been whittled away by all those hurtful accusations, until all that was left were foggy memories of happier times. She had gone back to Edinburgh and moved in with a close friend from college days, no doubt painting as dark a portrait of James as possible to anyone who would listen.

He thinks of this likely scenario as he picks up the little package tied expertly with string, acknowledging the fact that he had probably hurled as many twisted words in Louise's direction as she had in his. What could she possibly want after three years apart? The object bears only his name, written in Louise's unmistakable hand, and James notices that there is no stamp. He shudders at the realisation that it must have been delivered by hand during the night. Does this mean that Louise has moved back to Oxford?

James fetches a knife from the kitchen and sits at the table, curious as to what might be inside. The string is of that thick and hairy type, seemingly unnecessary for such an insignificant-looking item. James slices through the knotted strands to the brown paper beneath, then unfolds the wrapping to reveal a navy-blue cardboard box.

He slowly takes off the lid, places it on the table and looks inside the small container. Within is a glass vial of purple liquid, secured by a faded cork and cushioned on a bed of maroon silk.

James's curiosity quickly turns to frustration. Why had Louise not enclosed a note of some kind, bearing a clue as to what this stuff was, or what he was supposed to do with it?

'Bloody typical! Playing games like you always did and making me look like a fool. Well, not this time, *darling!* Not this....'

James is about to pick up the little bottle, intent on throwing it against the wall in anger, when he notices a corner of something white, sticking out of the silk lining. His interest returns after he removes the tiny card, for he can see that there are words written upon it. James puts on his glasses, and squints slightly to determine the three-word inscription, again written by Louise. It reads:

DON'T DRINK ME

James lets out a dismissive laugh, convinced that his former partner is up to her old tricks again, this time sowing seeds of confusion through subterfuge.

'Come on, you must think I'm really stupid, Louise! Well, just to spite you and for old time's sake, I'm going to ignore your little instruction and drink this down right now!'

As she knew he would, James immediately takes the cork from the vessel and tips its purple contents down his throat. He falls writhing and twisting to the floor and is dead within five minutes.

~~~~

Louise had taken a midnight stroll down Byron Road earlier in the week. She wore a black anorak with the hood up and was pleased to see his car parked outside the block of flats. On her return at 2.00 a.m. on the 15th, Louise sneaked down the side alley and slipped the package through the communal letterbox.

Now, in her new flat, Louise imagines James's final death throes and the empty box and bottle close by. She takes pleasure in the delicious fantasy of asking him one last question:

'I never told you that my middle name was Alice, did I, James?'

AN UNWELCOME RETURN

A conference room on the twenty-first floor of a modern office block in the centre of Manchester. Twelve high-powered executives at 'Nielsen Fox' are discussing the minutiae of an important trade deal, via a video link with the CEO in Copenhagen. All is going well, until one in the group starts to feel distinctly uncomfortable. He covers his mouth with his left hand and starts to speak as quietly as possible.

'Oh no, not you, not NOW! Just piss off, why don't you?'
'Well that's not a very nice welcome, is it, Stephen?'
'You're not *welcome*, that's why!'
'Ask me politely and I might just disappear again.'
'OK, OK! Mr. Bubbles, go away.'
'How about a 'please'?'
'Mr. Bubbles, go away, *please!*'
'That's much better, Stephen, but.... I've decided to stay.'

Steve Bailey, Head of Communications, tries hard to ignore his imaginary friend, last encountered over thirty years ago, and tries to concentrate on the presentation. This proves to be impossible, mainly because Mr. Horatio Bubbles is now standing in front of the screen and frantically waving, blocking Steve's view.

Steve shuffles in his seat, gesturing as discreetly as possible for the uninvited guest to step aside. His urgent, dismissive hand movements are ignored by Mr. Bubbles, but are noticed by one of his colleagues. She looks directly at him and raises a quizzical eyebrow, before returning her attention to the ongoing interaction with Denmark.

Mr. Bubbles joyfully whips out his bubble-blowing pipe, at which point Steve realises that this whole situation must stop. He clears his throat to get everyone's attention, including that of Mr. Bubbles.

'I wish to apologise to everyone, and especially to you, Henrik, but I'm not feeling too well and need to take a comfort break. Sorry.'

'That's fine, Steve. Go and get some fresh air. We've got all the details pretty much sorted so, unless there are any more questions, we can probably close the meeting. Anyone?'

The question is met with silence, much to Steve's relief. Mr. Bubbles claps his hands with glee and hops from foot to foot, knowing he will soon be given his erstwhile friend's undivided attention.

Steve leaves the room and heads straight for the car park with Mr. Bubbles skipping alongside him, blowing bubbles all the way.

'Can you stop doing that, please? You *know* that they can be seen in the real world, so someone's sure to notice!'

'Why should I care, Stephen? Besides, it's what I do!'

'Alright, if you must, but we need to have a serious talk!'

Towards the back of the car park, Steve pushes his childhood creation against the trunk of a large sycamore growing near the fence and takes a moment to look at Mr. Bubbles. He is dressed exactly as Steve remembers him – a peacock blue suit with a yellow bubble motif, hat and shoes made of bubble wrap and a large nose like a clown's, although Horatio's is transparent. Mistakenly thinking that no-one is watching from the office block (eighteen people on five different levels are, including seven in his department), he starts his remonstrations.

'What the fuck are you doing here? Why turn up now after all this time, and did it really have to be during that important meeting?'
'I've just been so lonely, Stephen. You never draw me anymore, you never call my name, you never sing our little 'bubble' song, so I thought I'd remind you that I still exist. I'll *always* exist, Stephen.'
'Are you threatening me, Bubbles? Because if you are, I can just walk away and ignore you forever.'
'Ah, but that's surely the point. You can't, can you? I'm a part of your childhood, a childhood so lonely that you felt a need to create me in the first place. Oh, Stephen, remember all the fun we had together, laughing and playing in our own little world!'
'That was when I was eight! I've grown up, in case you hadn't noticed, and please don't call me Stephen again. I'm known here as Steve.'
'You'll always be that pathetic little cry baby to me, *Stephen,* and I want to play some more! You *will* do as I say!'
'Well, we'll see about that, Bubbles!'

On the 21st floor, most of Steve's colleagues are now looking down at the car park, including his manager, Caroline Webster. They watch as 'Nielsen Fox's Head of Communications shouts at the trunk of a large tree. His arms are flailing amidst a mass of bubbles, and he intermittently punches his head in what appears to be intense frustration.

Steve Bailey's team-mates point and laugh at the strange behaviour below, all except for Caroline, who silently moves away from the window.

THE SUBJECT

We eavesdrop on two figures in a certain Italian artist's studio, several centuries ago. One is seated and calm, whereas the other appears rather unsettled.

'Erm....'

'What?'

'I was wondering if you could just....'

'Just *what*?'

'Well.... smile a little more normally, perhaps?'

'I don't see how or why I should. I mean, this *is* my smile. What's wrong with it?'

'Nothing.... really. It's just a bit quirky, that's all.'

'It's a quirk I'm rather proud of if you don't mind! Besides, I thought that was what you wanted when you asked me up here. If I recall, your exact words were 'Come up and see my etchings and I'll make it worth your while.' I assumed you meant that you'd like to paint me and that the main draw, so to speak, was my enigmatic facial expression!'

'Enigmatic? I'm not sure I'd use *that* word to describe it.'

'I'm sure people will in the future when they see your painting. They'll stare at it and wonder what the subject was thinking about during this very sitting. Indeed, I've a strong feeling they'll never be quite sure about her identity, either.'

'What do you mean?'

'Well, *maybe* it will be of me, the wife of the moderately successful merchant, Francesco del Giocondo. He's *planning* to commission you to paint my portrait, but he hasn't got around to it yet. I just happened to be passing by when you saw me shopping for oranges in the market. Another possibility is that you'll base it on your mother, Caterina, or even that it will be of *you* disguised as a woman.... but we won't go *there*.'

'Well, at least tell me your first name.'

'I'll give you a choice of three. I might be Louise, Lisa or Eloise, but you have to guess which one. I'm rather enjoying this game!'

'This is no game! I'm a serious artist so, *whoever* you are, could we just get on with it, please?'

'Alright, alright! How about this? Is this smile more what you're after?'

'Now you're just being silly. That's just a stupid grin! Perhaps try looking more earnest instead.'

'Like this?'

'No, NO! Right, that's enough. This sitting is over!'

'Why?'

'*Why*? Because.... because now you just look like a complete and utter moaner, Lisa!'

THE RED ROOM

Aidan had fallen in love with the third-floor apartment in Grosvenor Crescent as soon as he stepped inside. The spacious rooms! The high ceilings! The rent was higher than his place in Alberta Road, but not so much as to be unaffordable. He would just have to tighten his belt until his promised promotion was confirmed, due to take effect in two months' time.

Nick, the letting agent, sorted the tenancy's paperwork in a matter of days, much to Aidan's surprise and satisfaction. The flat suited his needs perfectly, apart from one aspect set out in the agreement, namely that the décor was not to be changed. Most of the walls were painted in inoffensive colours, but the room at the end of the hallway strangely unnerved him.

It seemed odd to Aidan that *anyone* would choose to decorate a room in such a fashion. The walls, the curtains, the carpet, even the ceiling - everything was red! The predominant shade was one of deep crimson, but other tones served to accentuate the oppressive atmosphere, ranging from intense scarlet to ruby. In the centre of the room sat an armchair upholstered in leather of a dark cherry, slightly scuffed in places.

The mantelpiece, painted the same shade of maroon as the fireplace, had only three ornaments placed upon it. These comprised a goblet fashioned from garnet-coloured glass, a Chinese vase bearing vermillion, flame-eating dragons and a delicate porcelain bowl, patterned with an interlocking motif, detailed in brick red. There were two shelves of books to the left of the hearth, and every volume was bound in leather of a burgundy hue, aged and worn. The rest of the flat was fully furnished, so it seemed peculiar to Aidan that there were so few adornments in *that* room.

During the first three months, the new tenant barely entered the red space, finding the interior somewhat claustrophobic. Gradually, however, Aidan felt drawn not only to step inside, but also to spend increasing amounts of time there. After the first few occasions, he noticed that the crimson walls had softened to a more welcoming toffee apple hue, and that the deep pile mahogany carpet was a lighter shade than before.

The room began to exert a magnetic hold over him. Each time Aidan was about to leave the flat, he would feel drawn back along the hallway and compelled to open the pillar box red door.

Whilst seated in the armchair one evening, Aidan felt something soft tickling his nose. Looking up, he was amazed to see flurries of red rose petals floating down from the scarlet ceiling. As they continued to fall, he stretched out his arms and started to laugh uncontrollably, accepting the room's embrace.

~~~~

Two weeks later. 09:40.

'Aidan Mitchell speaking.'
'Hello? Is that you, Aidan?'
'Who is this?'
'It's Erin! You're on my creative team, remember?'
'Oh, right. Of course.'
'This is the fifth time this month you've not come into the office and I'm sick of covering for you.'
'I.... I have to be at home today.'

'What for? If it's a delivery, can't your neighbours take it in for you?'

'No.... it's nothing like that. I just....'

'I don't want to know, *colleague*, but I'll tell you one thing. Huw is so angry with you that he's thinking of giving your promotion to Ross instead. Did you hear that? Aidan?'

But Aidan hadn't heard. He was already moving towards the red door, having deliberately dropped his phone en route.

By that stage, the only time the room allowed its willing captive to leave the apartment was to visit the large supermarket on Waterman Street, but even there its influence was growing.

Red peppers and tomatoes, red chillies and red onions, strawberries and raspberries, steak and beef mince, Shiraz and Ruby Port. The red space dictated Aidan's shopping habits and he ate all his meals in the room, swilled down with wine straight from the bottle. Any meat on his plate was always raw, as it would lose its colour if cooked, which would never do.

Eventually, even Aidan's shopping trips were curtailed by the red room's hold over him. The food ran out in less than a week, after which he just sat staring at the walls, ever compliant but weakened by hunger.

~~~~

Now, on the morning of what will be his last day, Aidan is vaguely aware of rapid knocks at the front door, interspersed with shouting. Huw has had enough of his employee's non-attendance and, although deeply frustrated, feels a level of concern.

Aidan's only focus is to fetch a glass of water and return to the red room, this action having been permitted. Due to the lack of sustenance his movements are sluggish, so the noise outside has ceased by the time Aidan finishes shuffling back along the hallway.

Realising that a neighbour must have buzzed Huw in and satisfied that his boss has now gone, Aidan pushes open the red door. All thoughts evaporate, however, as soon as he sees the changes that have taken place within the room since he left it, barely ten minutes ago.

Every three-dimensional object has flattened itself against the walls, appearing more like paintings set into the crimson surface. The armchair has moved next to the altered fireplace and is just completing its metamorphosis, the last of the dark cherry leather being subsumed into the walls with ease. Once Aidan is inside the room, the red door slams shut and traps him there, before it becomes the last element to yield to two dimensions. He stares incredulously at the walls as the paintwork turns from toffee apple to blood red, whilst moving from matt to a high gloss finish.

A slight creak followed by others. A disturbance of dust.

Surely it can't be true. Aidan rubs his eyes but, unfortunately, they have *not* deceived him. The walls that housed the fireplace and the door are slowly but inexorably moving together. Aidan watches in terror as the blood red paint begins to run down the walls, covering everything as it travels.

The mahogany carpet deepens in colour, loses its soft texture and transforms itself into a coagulating layer of red blood cells and plasma, holding Aidan's feet fast in its unyielding grip. Sudden tears prick his eyes as he realises that the room has gradually tricked him, imposing its will upon his mind, but why?

The more Aidan struggles the faster the space diminishes so, in a matter of minutes, he feels both walls touching his clothes. At first the sensation is strangely intimate, even slightly comforting, but soon the increasing pressure floods his brain with dread. Aidan was facing the flattened fireplace when the blood carpet took hold, but the suffocating walls now force his head sideways as they crush him further.

Aidan feels the breath forced out of his body and gasps for air. Muscle pain rips through him and his lungs collapse in on themselves. His other internal organs rupture as skin breaks open, and fresh blood immediately seeps into the glossy walls. Aidan's eyeballs burst and his brain erupts into mush. His bones and teeth powder into dust, sticking to the walls as they close together.

The fully replenished walls move back and return the room to its original dimensions, adopting the innocent, toffee apple shade as they settle. The nutrient-rich, glutinous pool recedes, and tufts of the deep pile carpet rise again. They silently reclaim the area, cushioning a set of keys, now all that remains of Aidan. Finally, every object becomes three dimensional once more, and the stage is set for the next unsuspecting tenant.

~ ~ ~ ~

'So, are you interested, Mia?'
'Oh, definitely, Nick. This flat would be ideal for me, and there's much more space than I'm used to. I do have one question, though.'
'Yes?'

'Why did the last tenant leave? It's just something I always ask when I'm taking on a new place.'

'Sure. I think he moved away, Mia. It was all rather sudden. I didn't actually speak to Mr. Mitchell before he went, but he left his keys here, so he clearly wasn't thinking of coming back.'

'Bit odd.'

'I suppose, but the flat's yours now, once I get the paperwork sorted out. I should have it ready by Friday, so drop by the office then.'

'Great! Thank you so much, Nick.'

'My pleasure. I'll just lock up.'

Nick ushers Mia out of the apartment and politely asks her to start walking downstairs. Once she is out of sight, he casts a single glance at the red door at the end of the hallway and smiles. It is a smile both of union and continuity. Through the blooded bond established with the room, he is always made aware when feeding has finished. Every time, after those strange shudders in his stomach cease, Nick knows it is safe to visit the flat and remove the latest victim's belongings.

The agent closes the front door, turns the key and whistles as he hurries to catch up with the new tenant. In anticipation of an imminent source of fresh food, a slight tremor ripples around the red walls before they settle again into silence.

NOTORIOUS CROOKS RIDE AGAIN?

A young woman emerges from the kitchen with two mugs of hot chocolate. She sets them down on the low, beer-stained table in front of her boyfriend, who is transfixed by something on the television.

'What you watchin'?'
'A film about a couple of gangsters.'
'Looks borin'.'
'No, it's good! They robbed loads of places and everyone was proper scared of 'em and that. They were literally real. It's not made up.'
'OK, what were they called, then?'
'Er.... Bonnie and Clyde.'
'Never 'eard of 'em, although....'
'What?'
'They sound a bit like *our* names.'
'How do you mean?'
'Well, Bonnie and Clyde, Zoe and Lloyd....'
'Oh, yeah! We could be like them! Robbin' and nickin' stuff, on the run from town to town!'
'Just think. You could get enough cash to buy that guitar you've always wanted!'
'Yeah, babe, and you could get all made up, like one of them film stars!'
'Let's do it! We've got nothin' to lose and it'll be a right laugh!'
'No, this is serious, Zoe. It's got to be done right, so pass me that pizza box. We can draw a map on the lid, once we decide who our first target is gonna be.'
'First of many, my criminal mastermind, first of many!'

~ ~ ~ ~

BUNGLED RAID CAUSES HILARITY

Two people were arrested after a raid on an off-licence went wrong. Zoe Parker, 21, and Lloyd Barrow, 23, both of Winchester Road, burst into 'Corker Wines' on Hamilton Street at 7.23 p.m., brandishing nothing more than unconvincing revolver-shaped water pistols and an attitude problem.

During their frantic but nervous shouts of 'Stick 'em up!' and 'Nobody messes with Zoe and Lloyd!', the owner, Mr. Tomasz Kominski, calmly pressed the button underneath his counter, alerting the police. When officers arrived, they found the 'arch criminals' spraying each other with shaken up cans of lager, jumping up and down on crisp packets and shouting 'YOUR FAULT! YOUR FAULT!'

Before they were led away, Mr. Kominski made them clean up their mess and pay for the stock they had damaged. He told our reporter that he hoped the court would make an example of the hopeless pair. Smiling broadly, he added:

'I mean, what were they going to do? Squirt me to death?'

KEYS TO LIFE

Geraldine sat in her rocking chair, looking out at her large garden. The hollyhocks were beautiful this year, stately yet showing off at the same time. She closed her eyes and drifted into a memory when she managed everything herself and had no need of Robert's help, although nowadays she was always glad of the young gardener's company.

She turned ninety-four in July, defiant in her wish to stay in the house rather than 'rot in some hideous care home' as she put it, whenever the subject came up with her children. The thought of such an establishment broke through her reverie, and she opened her eyes to find a bunch of keys on the small, ornate table beside her. Puzzled, she gave voice to her thoughts.

'Wherever did *they* come from? They're not mine and Robert's the only person who's been here lately. I don't understand....'

Geraldine absentmindedly lifted the keys off the table and felt an immediate shudder down her spine. Unnerved, she settled back in her chair, and studied the keys one by one. Two were broken, snapped off halfway down the shank and rendered useless, but the others were intact. Geraldine's eyes were drawn towards the keyring and she was amazed to find her initials imprinted in the metal. She ran a wrinkled finger over the letters and muttered to herself.

'G.S.W. – I wonder why they're written on here.'
'The reason, Geraldine Sarah Winters, is that we are the keys to your life. Look more closely and let us explain.'

Geraldine, startled by the voice, threw the bunch of keys onto the table. She stared at them for a moment and then asked a question.

'Am I going mad?'
'No. You acknowledged us when you touched your initials. Now, pick us up again and study the wooden key first.'

Geraldine did as she was told, then smiled at a warm memory.

'It's like one from the set my father gave me when I was seven years old! He made them for me to play with and I remember pretending that they could open any lock, anywhere in the world! How I miss him. Such a kind man.'

Geraldine reminisced in silence for a while, but then the keys began to speak again, telling her to look at the next on the ring.

'Ah yes! I received one just like this on my twenty-first birthday! How did that old song go? *She's got the key to the door, never been twenty-one before....*'

The old woman felt a certain bitter-sweetness, happy with the warm recollection, yet wishing she could be that age again. The voice of the keys cut through the memory with a new request.

'Observe the next two keys, if you will.'
'Why are these ones broken? I noticed them earlier.'
'Think about your first two serious relationships in your late twenties, Geraldine. Those men caused you so much pain.'
'Yes, they did. When Kenneth broke off our engagement I was devastated, especially when he

revealed his affair with my sister. Roger gradually taught me to believe in love again, but he just disappeared one evening, leaving me heartbroken for the second time. I never saw him again. What a fool I was!'

Geraldine started to cry. The keys waited patiently for her to recover, before introducing the penultimate object on the circle of metal.

'So, who does this complete key represent, Geraldine?'

'It must be my wonderful Harold! What a great husband he was, and the perfect remedy for my heartache. Oh, and the next one looks exactly like the large key to the farmhouse kitchen door. We had such happy times living there, watching the children growing up, playing in the woods and having picnics together.'

'All things must end, however, happy *or* sad. We know you understand this now, Geraldine. Look at the ring again.'

'There are no more keys! Why are there no more keys?'

'We are the markers of your life. A long and interesting one, yes, but now it must end.'

'Please! Not yet! Surely this can't be my last day! Are there really no more of you?'

A brief pause.

'There is one last key. Look, there on the carpet near the door.'

Geraldine turned to her right to see a key, fashioned from white bone, and a question rose in her confused mind.

'Why isn't that one with *you*?'

'You must reach for it, Geraldine, then you will understand.'

'But I can't, not without getting down on the floor.'

'We insist that you try.'

Geraldine, full of curiosity but scared of falling, pushed her frail body up from the rocking chair and tried to steady herself. She managed this for a few moments, but then tumbled forwards, terrible pain spreading through her weak frame on contact with the ground. The keys, which were still in her hand, urged her on.

'Grab the bone key, Geraldine, then hold it! Hold it!'

She obeyed their demand and, as her fingers closed around the skeleton key, a life filled with joyful times and painful sorrows ebbed away.

MEDUSA IN THE EAST END

London, 2019. She lifts her head off the pillow, taking care not to rouse them. They are all coiled in deep sleep, but she knows she must act quickly before they awaken. Moving slowly, she gingerly collects the little bodies from the many traps set around the filthy flat and places them in a pile on the stained floorboards. It isn't long before her charges' tongues taste the blood in the air, and they open their eyes wide in anticipation.

She feeds a small furry corpse to each one in turn then sits back on the faded sofa, knowing that they will sleep after feasting to aid their digestion. Being immortal, she needs no such sustenance, but must keep her only companions in top, shiny-scaled condition. As she waits for their contented writhing to cease, she looks at the mould-streaked walls. It is early morning, but the July sunshine is already flooding the squalid, rodent-infested flat on the seventeenth floor.

She glances at the stone figure in the corner, frozen in shock and collecting dust. The woman had peculiar tastes in clothes (not a flowing white robe in sight), but the new 'owner' needs *something* to wear when venturing outside. Part of her outfit is a large floppy sunhat, the wide brim shadowing her face when her head is lowered.
She gets dressed an hour later, then gently secures the hat in place, choosing to ignore the soft hisses of complaint from underneath.

Out in the park, she indulges her only pleasure in this lonely existence. Her first victim annoys her by pushing past, oblivious to his surroundings and constantly staring down at something. She shouts a few words to get his attention, lifts her head when he looks up, then simply walks away from the scene, leaving a new stone sculpture in her wake.

She thinks back to one occasion when amusement also raised its head, a sensation she had not encountered before. Finding herself in something called a 'garden centre', she used her powers to produce original statuary, then placed her creations amongst those for sale. She rested awhile on a convenient bench nearby, during which time she noticed an elderly woman intensely studying one of the new pieces. Moving closer, she listened in to the ensuing conversation with the husband:

'Look at this one, Stan! She's the spitting image of Barbara at No. 47!'
'You're right, Jean, but that's impossible. She never mentioned she'd done any modelling work.'
'Well, let's go and ask her on the way home. Come on.'

The couple moved away, scratching their heads, and the sculptress smiled with her face in shadow.

There was no such fun to be had today, however, so after a few hours of ultimately unsatisfying transformations, she returns home, bored and tired. The lift isn't working, so she trudges up the concrete stairs and removes her sunhat when she enters the fetid hallway.

She will reset the traps when the sun sinks behind the apartment blocks. Later, in bed, her writhing companions will coil and settle on the pillow. Sleep will eventually take hold but, as on so many nights, the question of how she came to be in this dirty city, and in a time so far from her own, will stalk her dreams.

ONE PAY CHEQUE AWAY

In the shadow of a castle on a wide city street, three figures have taken shelter in a porch beneath a large stone archway. On their way there, the steady summer drizzle had made their blankets smell of damp, long-forgotten basements and now they watch as the rain gradually darkens the concrete. A greasy, half-eaten burger scents the air and a polystyrene container spews limp chips onto the pavement. A man in a long black cloak stops in front of the men and dramatically clears his throat to get their attention. When no-one looks up, he tries to start a conversation.

'How do you do? Would you mind if I put these carrier bags down for a moment? They're quite heavy, you see, and I haven't stopped running since I.... since I.... well, since I left. Would that be alright?'

The stranger receives barely a shrug from the group, so assumes that nobody cares either way. He sets the three carriers down and flexes his fingers, waiting for someone to speak. Eventually someone does.

'Not seen you around here before.'
'No, you won't have done, but I assure you I *am* local.'

The cloaked newcomer vaguely waves a gloved hand towards the castle, but no-one takes any notice. After another long pause, he tentatively asks a question.

'Is.... anybody hungry?'
'Always! What are you offering?'

The figure rummages in one of the bags, pulls out three large jam tarts and hands them out. They are devoured in under a minute and, with his beard specked with pastry crumbs, one of the men speaks of a just-stirred memory.

'These are almost as good as mine! My name's Nick. I used to run a successful bakery a few streets away, but the gambling bug bit me hard and I spiralled down into debt. I lost everything in a few weeks, and that's how I ended up here. Tell him what happened to you, Dan.'

'Alright. Well, things were good for a while. I worked in finance and enjoyed a comfortable family life, but I found I was spending more and more time in the office due to my increasing workload. When I was made redundant, the mortgage fell into arrears and my wife left with the kids. I suffered bouts of depression and now this is all I have.'

'That's terrible!'

The stranger is shocked to hear of such personal tragedy and turns to the third individual to hear *his* story.

'Like Dan, my life fell apart when my marriage broke down. I became homeless, but I did manage to keep my job going for a while. I pretty much lived out of my car for a couple of months. I was too ashamed to let my boss know my situation, but then a colleague saw me searching bins for food and told her, so I got the sack. I'm John, by the way. What's *your* name?'

'Oh, I'm Jack. Am I right to assume that none of you ever thought you'd be living like this?'

The three men slowly shake their heads in silence, and Jack feels an urgent need to help in some way. He is not being entirely selfless, however, as he can hear the shouts of the Queen's soldiers further down the street, but a plan has already formed in his nimble mind.

'Look, I really need a place to hide for a few hours. Please can I share your shelter?'

Jack must make his pitch quickly, for now he can see the royal guards pushing past people as they move ever closer. He takes off his cloak with a flourish and reveals his bright livery of blue and gold, patterned throughout with a red heart motif (he had hidden his heart-emblazoned hat in one of the carrier bags). Nick, Dan and John gasp in amazement.

'Please help me! I'm on the run and in grave danger - but see what I have for you!'

The men watch as Jack empties out the bags onto the dry area beneath the arch. High-crusted, savoury pies tumble out, along with roasted meats and fruit-filled pastries.

'Hide me quickly, then we can feast together later!'

The men glance at each other and nod, then hurriedly refill the carriers with the tempting food, along with Jack's hat. They stand up and push Jack behind them so that he cannot be seen. All are nervous when the soldiers approach the archway and listen as their leader speaks.

'He has to be around here somewhere, men. The Queen will go *mad* if we return empty-handed, so come on!'

The soldiers hurry past the street-dwellers, ignoring them as so many others have done. Nick waits a few moments before telling Jack that the coast is clear.

'Thank you for your kind assistance. You are clearly good people. Now, eat whatever you like!'

'Let's pace ourselves. There's enough food here for at least two days.'

'I have gold ingots, too! Please take them, for I've had enough of this privileged life and I want to live amongst ordinary folk. Your stories of hardship have moved me deeply, and....'

Jack stops speaking, having noticed that the soldiers are returning. He pushes himself behind his new friends and waits for the Queen's men to pass by. They trudge past looking anxious and defeated, aware of the fate that awaits them at the castle.

Jack re-emerges wearing a broad grin, relieved to have evaded capture. He smiles at Nick, Dan and John, happy to have found such good hearts out on the street. In turn, they share out the small gold bars, already thinking of a brighter future.

HOW TO AMUSE A MUSE (OR NOT)

In a West End theatre, the last member of the audience has just left, following a first night performance. Earlier, the plush, scarlet curtains had closed with a smooth, velvety swoosh, but now the usual argument begins.

'Well, that was a load of rubbish.'

'What do you mean? I thought it was really good!'

'It was absolutely puerile and a complete waste of two hours.'

'How can you say that? There were some excellent jokes and the whole piece was light-hearted and fun!'

'That's all that matters to you, isn't it? If it's full of jokes and *fun* you're happy, but then I suppose you can't be any other way, really.'

'Exactly, in the same way you're never satisfied unless the play's full of doom and gloom. I wish you'd lighten up a little, Melpy, for it would do you good!'

'It would do me anything but good to 'lighten up'. You know I can't stand froth and nonsense, and I also can't stand it when you shorten my name!'

'OK, OK, Melpomene. I only do it to annoy you, but it does work every time!'

'You always have to make a joke about everything, Thalia. Life isn't full of laughter, you know.'

'But it's not full of misery, either! You must admit that everyone around you really enjoyed themselves this evening.'

'No, not everyone. When I turned to look at the audience, I saw several people – what did you say it was called – 'texting'?'

'I think so, from what I've overheard. They were probably 'texting' their friends to say how much they were loving the show.'

'Or much more likely telling them not to waste their money on such a dreadful play!'

'Well, when *I* turned around, all I could see were happy, smiling faces. Surely that's better than frowns and furrowed brows everywhere!'

'At least in the plays *I* like, deep subjects are explored, and nothing is played for cheap laughs.'

'Subjects like death, sorrow and pain, you mean?'

'Yes, and what's wrong with that? Better to have a bit of substance than mere whimsy!'

'Give it a rest, Miss Misery! Look, we'll just have to agree to disagree as usual, Melpomene. Let's face it, that's all we've ever done and all we will ever do.'

'I agree, Thalia. There's no point in trying to mask the truth.'

Thalia giggles and wonders whether Melpomene has seen the joke. Even if she has, she would be unable to show it, due to her constantly downturned mouth. As on so many occasions, the spirits of these Greek goddesses had temporarily inhabited audience members, after sweeping down into the stalls to enjoy or endure the performance. Every time, after each play has finished, they return to their forms above the proscenium arch to critique what they have just seen. Tragedy or comedy – it hardly matters because they know that one muse will be amused and the other will not. Despite this eternal dispute, however, they always agree on *one* thing:

THE SHOW MUST GO ON!

LIKE AN UNUSED COFFIN

In sheer anger and defiance, Imogen lifts her black suitcase and hurls it with all her strength against the back of the plush, red-striped sofa. Clive doesn't show the slightest reaction and continues to stare into the flames as they dance in the large fireplace. Outside the snow is swirled around by the howling, whistling wind. In normal circumstances, such weather would command attention, but tonight the real drama is happening indoors.

'What the hell is wrong with you? I told you this morning that I would be leaving tonight, and you've made no attempt to stop me. Don't these past five years mean anything? Clive? CLIVE!'

When Clive doesn't respond, Imogen screams loudly and kicks a nearby chair. She picks up her suitcase, takes it through to the hall, then composes herself before returning to face her husband. She stands between him and the fireplace, determined to have her final say.

'This is your last chance, Clive, because as soon as my brother gets here, I'm off forever! I used to find your cool detachment appealing, but I've come to realise you're like an unused coffin, wooden and empty, and I just can't bear it anymore!'

Still no response. Imogen continues, struggling to hold back tears borne of frustration.

'You're like a closed book to me, Clive. I'm begging you, please! Show some emotion, show some feeling and I'll text Gus and tell him to turn back, but do SOMETHING!'

Clive briefly looks into her imploring eyes, offers a slight smile, then gazes at the flames again. He slowly stands, and Imogen is surprised to see a tear trickle down his left cheek.

He faces her now with his arms at his side, rigid and completely motionless, and Imogen is amazed to see that his skin and clothes are patterning with wood grain. Within minutes his body transforms into a wooden sarcophagus, roughly painted and low on detail. A thin line reveals itself, running from head to toe, before widening slightly. Imogen watches in horror as Clive forces his arms to move. Clearly in considerable pain, he pushes his fingers into the narrow space and begins to prise himself apart. His grained body groans and his spine creaks with complaint, but Clive knows that the suffering is necessary for his wife to understand.

Shocked and confused, Imogen steps forward to look inside her husband's hollow shell, and what she finds within changes everything. Gently hovering inside him is a leather-bound book, with a golden heart embossed on the clasp. Imogen reaches inside and lifts it out to take a closer look. She tentatively releases the fastening and slowly opens the volume, then catches her breath at the very first line she reads, displayed there in Clive's unmistakeable handwriting:

I LOVE HER, BUT I DON'T KNOW HOW TO TELL HER.

SHE MEANS THE WORLD TO ME, BUT I AM UNABLE TO SHOW IT.

EVEN IF I TOOK HER TO THE MOST BEAUTIFUL, MOST ROMANTIC PLACES ON EARTH, LIKE VENICE, PARIS OR VIENNA, THE WORDS OF LOVE STILL WOULDN'T FLOW FROM MY LIPS.

I MUST APPEAR HEARTLESS AND INDIFFERENT, BUT I'M TERRIFIED THAT IF I TRY TO EXPLAIN MY FEELINGS, I'LL MESS IT UP AND SHE'LL LAUGH AT ME BEFORE LEAVING ME ALONE.

I SIMPLY COULDN'T BEAR THAT, WATCHING MY WORLD COLLAPSE AS SHE CLOSES THE FRONT DOOR BEHIND HER.

I AM NOTHING WITHOUT HER, YET MY REMOTENESS MAKES ME NOTHING TO HER, SO I AM NOTHING EITHER WAY.

NOTHING TO HER EVERYTHING, IN OTHER WORDS.

I AM CAPTIVE IN A PRISON OF MY OWN MAKING AND EVEN HER LOVE CANNOT SAVE ME.

Imogen reads the words again. In opening himself up to her, both literally and emotionally, Clive's life has ended. His words of love were expressed far too late, however, for his wife's affections lay elsewhere and have for some time.

Frustrated and angry, Imogen hurls the book into the fire, then smashes Clive's effigy with a heavy poker. It takes just under an hour for Imogen to feed the splintered body to the flames. Now, with the task completed, she sits on the sofa, a thin smile crossing her lips as a new plan takes shape.

Gus had offered to let her stay at his apartment while she 'sorted herself out', but why not go straight to Simon? After all, they had discussed living together often enough.

She excitedly texts Simon:

COME TO THE HOUSE NOW! I'M READY TO BE WITH YOU AND NEED TO GET AWAY TONIGHT. ALL LOVE IMMY XX

Simon messages back immediately with a large, beating heart emoji. Imogen grins, then texts her sibling:

THANKS FOR YOUR OFFER, GUS, BUT PLEASE GO BACK HOME. I'VE MADE OTHER ARRANGEMENTS AND I'LL BE IN TOUCH SOON. DON'T WORRY. I X

Imogen smirks, realising that she is sitting exactly where Clive had done, staring into the grate earlier in the evening. It had all worked out better than she could have imagined, albeit rather dramatically, and with no trace left of her dispassionate husband.

Twenty minutes later, she looks up on hearing a sound from outside. Simon swerves into the driveway, leaving semi-circular tracks in the wind-whipped whiteness.

THE STAR CUTTER

It started happening a week ago and has continued every night since. Could the cause be overtiredness? Louis had always got up at 4.00 a.m. to heat up the ovens and make fresh dough, so there had been no change in his routine. Might it be concern over the steady decline in customers coming into the shop, lured away by cheaper loaves in the recently opened supermarket? A worry, yes, but not yet enough to threaten his business of nearly forty years.

Louis sits at the kitchen table in the flat above the bakery, sipping a coffee and wishing he could discuss the recurring vision with Marie. His wife died ten years ago, taken by a devastating stroke. He misses her terribly and often speaks aloud to her as if she were still alive.

~~~~

In the first few months after Marie's passing, the only way Louis could function on a day-to-day basis was to immerse himself in the running of the bakery. He felt sure that Ben, who was nineteen at the time, found this approach also helped *him* with the grieving process, although father and son only acknowledged this to be true on the first anniversary of her death.

Three years ago, Ben decided to move to Canada and set up his own catering business. There he met Amelia and, in what seemed extreme haste to his father, got married in Vancouver after only knowing her for six months. Louis knew that *Marie* would never have begrudged them their happiness, but he just couldn't accept the situation somehow.

~~~~

Louis finishes his coffee and fleetingly wonders if calling Ben about the strange dreams might be a good idea, but he dismisses the thought just as quickly. The geographical distance was not the only deciding factor here, for an emotional chasm had spread between them after Ben's marriage to Amelia and they have hardly spoken since.

He could not even tell his employees, Nina and Sam, fearing they would at best laugh at him, and at worst think he had 'finally lost it'. No, he would just have to deal with this on his own.

The dream did not feel threatening in any way and was far from being a nightmare. It consisted of an odd landscape, completely formed from elements of Louis's longstanding expertise in the baking trade.

On the first night there were only hills, formed from an assortment of loaves arranged in rows and receding into the distance but, on the second occasion, Louis saw French sticks positioned at right angles to the bloomers, giving the impression of slender poplar trees.

Over the next four nights, flowers burgeoned in the foreground, each supported on a breadstick stem. Their centres were either pastel-shaded macaroons or doughnuts thickly coated in pink icing, with petals formed of filigree chocolate work, delicate and impressive.

During the night just passed, something rather different appeared in the navy-blue sky above the bakery landscape. Louis immediately recognised it, for these curved, buttery, viennoiserie pastries had always been popular with his customers. He woke up at 4.00 a.m. as usual and remembered the image, a smile creasing his stubbled face as he saw the joke.

'Not so much a crescent moon as a croissant moon. Ha! I like it!'

Throughout the day, Louis is increasingly distracted by thoughts of what might appear next. The nightly scene has become quite crowded and the only space left is next to the flaky moon.

Louis had left Nina to serve in the shop all morning, with Sam sulkily kneading and baking alone, and he only came downstairs during the lunchtime rush. Now, in the late afternoon, he finds himself rummaging through a dusty cardboard box in the kitchen, looking for.... what? Louis doesn't recall lifting it down from the shelf, yet here he is, frustrated and determined in equal measure.

He somehow knows the search is over (but not why) when he finds a five-pointed metal object, unused for many years, and lifts it out of the box. Louis examines the star cutter and passes it back and forth between his hands, fondly remembering that it belonged to Marie and that she was the last person to use it. He briefly wonders if the cutter is connected in some way to the nocturnal visions, but places the object on the kitchen table, sets the box back on the shelf and goes downstairs.

The baker ushers Nina and Sam out of the shop at 5.30 p.m. and thanks them for their help during the day. As he pushes the door shut, Louis can hear Sam grumbling about not getting paid enough as it is, without covering for the 'moody old sod'. With a sigh, he flips the card over from 'OPEN' to 'CLOSED', then climbs the stairs to his flat to endure another lonely evening.

Halfway through eating his dinner, Louis concedes that Sam is probably right. Over the past week, he must have appeared somewhat distant to his staff, distractedly going through the motions, and expecting them to deal with everything. As on so many occasions, he addresses his wife in the quiet space:

'I *will* make it up to them, Marie, I promise. They're hard workers and deserve to be rewarded, especially after this peculiar week.'

Louis picks up the star cutter and studies it intensely. The next thing he is aware of is staring down at the object, apparently having just placed it on his bedside table. He goes back to the lounge, where confusion ebbs and flows during the remainder of the evening, and Louis decides to 'call it a day' after the ten o'clock news.

The baker's landscape, now so familiar to Louis, looks the same as on the previous 'visit'. He feels a pang of disappointment, having grown to expect fresh additions on each occasion. During the day, he had imagined a sky festooned with biscuit stars, baked pale golden and contrasting beautifully with the curved moon, but the blue-black space holds nothing new.

Deep in sleep yet bidden by the vision, Louis stretches out his right hand and picks up Marie's star cutter. He slowly moves the metal shape to his chest and presses it over his heart, pushing down as hard as he can. As he holds it there, Louis sees two biscuit stars appear in the dream sky. In his final moments and with eyes still tightly closed, tears of joy stream down his face as he realises what is happening. He is at peace with Marie and the world at last, now left behind.

~ ~ ~ ~

Later in the morning, Sam will discover Louis's body and shout for Nina to come upstairs. Both will wonder about the star cutter, its positioning, and why their boss is wearing such a contented smile.

ROBINSON CLUELESS

The soft swish of palm trees along the shoreline. The gentle lapping of the warm waves on the pale sand. The intense blue of the cloudless sky. This place could only be described as idyllic, yet there is a new arrival here who has not even noticed its beauty. He appears extremely annoyed with something flat and rectangular held in his right hand, and continually jabs at it with his left index finger. Frustration boils over and he shouts at the sky.

'WHAT DOES IT TAKE TO GET A SIGNAL AROUND HERE?'

He throws the device onto the soft sand with a howl of anger and sits down in a complete sulk, unaware that he has been closely observed since he first appeared.

'Hey! What....?'

The castaway spins around after feeling a tap on his shoulder and finds himself looking at a heavily wrinkled, straggle-bearded face. Modern instincts kick in and he grabs his phone, his one and only possession in this beautiful place. Their eyes lock, each man assessing the potentially dangerous situation and deeply wary of the other. The new arrival decides to break the silence.

'Hi. My name is Peter Robinson, but all my friends call me Pete. I was wondering, is there anywhere I can get a coffee? I'd kill for a skinny latte right now!'

Bewildered eyes continue to stare back at him, and Peter realises that this is going to be a tough gig. He breaks away from the intense gaze and looks around for the first time.

'Wow! This place is amazing! I could take some great selfies here and my followers are going to be so jealous when they.... oh.'

Peter looks down at his phone, longing for it to function again. It doesn't. He realises that he hasn't eaten anything for a while, so he points to his mouth to indicate hunger. The old man nods his understanding and beckons Peter to stand. He leads him to one of the larger palms, where he removes a curved blade from his ragged clothing. Peter watches in amazement as the islander scales the tree in moments, and soon coconuts are softly thudding onto the beach. As soon as the expert climber's bare feet meet the sand, the clueless one asks a question.

'I'm pretty sure I've seen these online, but what do you *do* with them? I mean, I could look it up on my phone and.... oh.'

Still not speaking, the old man slices a coconut in two with a flash of his gleaming blade, allowing the water within to fall onto the sand. He then skilfully cuts away the fibrous husk and passes curved pieces of coconut flesh to the stranger.

'So *that's* how you do it! I'm impressed, buddy!'

Peter thought he saw his new companion wince at the remark, but he decides not to say anything. They sit on the sand and feast together in silence, during which another question rises in Peter's mind.

'Tell me, where exactly *are* we? It's just that whenever I travel, and I travel a lot, I like to let my friends and followers know my exact location.'

No answer comes, just the return of that relentless, wide-eyed stare, but Peter has an idea.

'Oh, wait! Don't worry, 'cos I can look it up on one of my apps and.... oh.'

Feeling totally dejected, Peter stares at his expensive trainers, and is surprised when a gnarled hand is placed upon his shoulder. He is even more surprised when the old man begins to speak.

'Look, Peter. I don't understand any of the terms you've been using or what that thing is that seems so important to you, but I can see that you're unhappy. Like you, I was washed ashore here, but long ago. I learnt to survive. I had to.'

The voice was clearly that of a fellow Englishman, faltering but full of empathy.

'You need to accept that there's no way off this island, but I can teach you all I know about the place. It's not so bad here once you get used to it. Besides, it'll be good to have some company, and you can tell me what I've missed out on since I arrived. My name was.... is.... Charles.'

They shake hands, and Peter looks at the wonderful setting that he must now call his home. He considers what will be a much simpler, less cluttered existence and revels in its instant appeal. He grabs his phone, stands up and runs towards the sea.

'I won't be needing *this* anymore, Charles!'

With a joyful laugh, Peter hurls the defunct object into the water. He returns to Charles, who is not at all happy.

'I don't really approve of you littering the sea like that, but it's done now, I suppose.'

Suitably chastened, Peter offers an explanation.

'I know, Charles, but I just wanted to free myself from it and what it represents. You really haven't missed much by not having one, you know.'

'You still haven't told me what it was called or *why* it was so important to you.'

'It doesn't matter now, believe me.'

'Alright, Peter. Let me show you the huts I've built. I've made three over the years, so you're welcome to use one until I teach you how to make your own.'

Charles stands up, then smiles for the first time.

'By the way, I don't usually let coconut water go to waste, but I'll show you how to pierce holes in the top and drink it fresh in future. Let's go and toast our new friendship with some now!'

'That sounds great, Charles, but please call me Pete from now on.'

'Very well, Pete. Just as long as you never call me 'buddy' again!'

The castaways gather the other coconuts and laugh as they walk towards the line of palms, away from the sand and surf.

BLIND EYES

Tommy Miracle took a long stretch on the bed in his cell and let out a deep sigh of satisfaction. It felt good that, after only two months, he had started to be respected on what he already saw as 'his' wing. This status had been achieved using surprisingly little violence, with none of it carried out by him, of course.

Tommy heard a key turn with the usual heavy clunk, but he didn't bother to move. He never showed respect for *any* 'screw' but, when *this* warden stood in front of him, something about his face made 'The Boss' feel uneasy.

'Miracle, stand up – NOW!'
'Alright, alright! Don't I.... know you from somewhere?'
'Shut it! STAND UP!'

Tommy grudgingly obeyed the order. He searched for a memory of the man but found nothing, so why did he seem familiar? The officer looked him up and down then smiled before continuing.

'Tommy Miracle, as I live and breathe. You won't have seen me in here before, but our paths crossed many years ago. I'm Chief Correctional Officer Williams. Gareth Williams. Don't recall anything? No? You disappoint me, Miracle, but allow me to refresh your memory.'

It appeared to Tommy that this official was relishing the situation. Why couldn't he remember where he had seen him?

'So.... cast your mind back to Greendale High School, Miracle. You were two years above me when I joined, and you targeted me from day one. Shoving my head down the toilet, pissing over my exercise books, waiting for me at the school gates every evening with your gang, making me hand over any money I had.... and one of your mates did this.'

That was it! The broken nose! The bully from Officer Williams's past smirked as recognition dawned, but he stopped when the warden spat in his face. Tommy was too shocked by the action to speak, let alone protest or retaliate in kind.

'I've been off sick for three months, but I returned to work a couple of days ago. On my first day back, my colleagues told me about our latest 'arrivals'. When your name came up, I could hardly believe it. It had to be you. I mean, how many Tommy Miracles are there?'

The prisoner did not answer. There was a power shift taking place and the scales of influence were now weighted in the officer's favour. Tommy could do nothing about it.

'I remember every morning when I trudged my way to school, wondering what fresh torment lay in store for me. I'm sure my work suffered because of your bullying and, as a result, my exam grades were totally crap. It took me *years* to feel confident about *anything* and I blame you for that miserable time, Miracle. To cap it all, my colleagues tell me you're doing the same thing here!'

Tommy's pride over his standing on the wing started to ebb away as he listened to his childhood victim.

'Well, it stops right now, Miracle, because *I'm* the one who controls what goes on around here, along with my fellow officers. You can't imagine how wonderful it feels to say that to your face after all these years!

'I'd say you'd be well-advised to watch your step over the coming weeks. There are plenty on this wing who already resent your rise and would be only too happy to put you in your place again. When, not if, something happens to you, Miracle, you can be sure that many a blind eye will be turned. Nobody will help you crawl back to your cell, however bloodied and bruised you are.'

Tommy Miracle - the bully, the tyrant - suddenly felt genuine fear, very much like the boy he had abused all those years ago. Chief Correctional Officer Williams turned towards the door, but then remembered another indignity from his schooldays and could not resist one last twist of the knife. He faced Tommy again with a question.

'Do you remember what you used to make me say, every time I handed over my money, Miracle?'

Silence.

'No? Well, let me remind you. It was 'Thank you, Lord Tommy'. If I refused, you'd get your idiots to throw me to the ground and give me a good kicking, as you stood there laughing. So now it's your turn, because you're going to thank *me* for the kicking *you'll* be getting soon. Well? What are you waiting for?'

'Thank you....'

'Sorry I didn't quite catch that, Miracle.'

'THANK YOU!'

'Better, but now address me properly!'

'THANK YOU, CHIEF CORRECTIONAL OFFICER WILLIAMS!'

'There, you see! That didn't hurt, did it? Everything will soon, though, but it's out of my hands as to exactly when. Take care, Miracle, and I really mean that.'

Officer Williams left the cell without another word, slammed the door hard and turned the key. Tommy Miracle, until very recently 'The Big Cheese', sat down on his bed, crushed and humiliated. This was going to feel like a much longer 'stretch' now, and a painful one, too.

CARDBOARD SLEEVES

April 2039. Five teenagers – Marky, Baz, Jen, Ed and Angie - stand outside a tired-looking old house, situated at the far end of the small town. The windows are filthy and there is a general feeling of decay and neglect.

'Go on, you knock!'
'Why should I, Baz?'
'Because, Marky, this was all your idea!'
'It's pretty creepy. Do you think someone actually lives inside, Jen?'
'Well there's one way to find out, Ed. Isn't there, *Marky*?'
'Alright. If no-one else will do it. Here goes....'

Angie laughs as Marky takes a deep breath and decisively knocks on the front door, so hard that several flakes of ancient paint fall onto the moss-edged top step. Nothing happens for a few moments, but then Jen notices that one of the yellowed net curtains in the front room has been drawn back slightly. It falls into its former position, after which the group hears keys being turned in locks. A chain is attached to its housing plate and nervous glances flash between them as the door slowly opens.

'Yes?'
'Er.... Hi. I was wondering.... well, we all were.... if you could show us some of your stuff from the old days. We've been given a school project called 'Life in the Past', and we thought you'd be the best person to ask around here.'

Marky holds back a smirk. Everyone in the town knows about the old weirdo who lives at the end of

Nelson Road and his hoarding, so there is bound to be loads of dusty old crap to look at inside.

The man runs his fingers through his tangled grey beard and looks at them individually, assessing the unexpected situation.

'Hmmm. I suppose you can come in if you don't mind the mess. I rarely get visitors, you see.'

The wary loner removes the chain and shuffles down the dingy hallway into the front room. The friends follow, quietly giggling and nudging each other. He pushes some old copies of music magazines off the threadbare sofa, then fetches two wooden chairs from the kitchen.

'Take a seat, all of you. My name's Bill, but don't bother telling me yours, because I've got a memory like a sieve.'

'Like a what?'

'Ah. I can see this could be quite hard work. Where to start? How about one of these?'

'It's just an old piece of cardboard!'

'Now that's where you're wrong, young lady. Let me show you what's inside.'

Bill carefully removes the inner sleeve and takes out the black disc. He smiles at his guests, but he is met with five puzzled stares.

'Surely you know what this is! Don't they sell these in record shops anymore?'

'Where?'

'This is how we used to listen to music! It's called a vinyl record.'

'No idea what you mean, mate. We stream ours – instant access and without the need for anything like that!'

'At least let me show you how it works, so that you can write about it in your project.'

As on so many occasions in the past, Bill places the disc on the turntable and moves the arm manually across to the outer edge. He gently lowers the needle and crackles start to spit from the speakers. The music begins, but is met with complete indifference from the visitors, so Bill tries to engage his already bored audience with more detail.

'My friends and I would spend hours studying the artwork on the covers, reading the sleeve notes and learning the lyrics. Great times.'
'Extremely dull times, more like! Now, what else have you got for us? Perhaps something we can actually *relate* to?'

Marky's tone of voice has changed, and Bill is beginning to feel uneasy. The old man nervously reaches for another object.

'I.... suppose I could show you this. It's a telephone.'
'That red thing? It looks nothing like ours! These days they're sleek and smart, unlike you, mate. When did you last have a bath? It reeks in here!'

Marky laughs, then offers his smartphone to Bill for closer inspection, but he refuses to even touch it.

'Oh no, thank you, but I must admit I did wonder what those things were that kept distracting you all.'
'Wow, you really *are* behind the times, mister! So how did this old thing work, then?'
'When I was your age, my parents had theirs on something called a 'telephone table'. It was situated in the hallway with a chair positioned nearby, to provide comfort for the person receiving, or making, a call.'

143

'Are you seriously telling me that you had to sit down and talk into.... which bit?'

'The receiver. This end here, look.'

'We take our phones with us everywhere! What about when you needed to make a call outside?'

'Ah! We had things called 'telephone boxes' for that. You'd open the door and step inside, then lift the receiver and dial the number. As soon as you heard the beeping noise, you'd push your loose change into the slot and start to speak.'

'Loose what?'

'Never mind. Oh, what about this? It was another way we used to listen to music. It's called a cassette tape and, as you can see, the tape is tightly wound around these two spools. When the first side had finished playing, you had to take it out of the machine and flip it over, although some *really* flashy ones played the second side without having to do that.'

Bill sees five pairs of eyes glazing over with disinterest, but he carries on talking anyway.

'What was great about these little beauties was that you could tape music off the radio! Mind you, sometimes the tape got mangled in the machine, so you had to carefully remove it from the....'

'Right! I think we've heard enough! We're going now.'

'But there's lots of other things to show you yet! Please stay. It's been nice to have some company for a change.'

Marky stands and moves closer to Bill. He looks the old man up and down, then smiles thinly before addressing him.

'Nah. Everything in this room is totally pathetic, just a load of useless rubbish. In fact, I reckon it should all be destroyed. Get rid of everything! What do you say, guys?'

He gives the slightest nod to his friends, who understand what the gesture means. All four stand up, grinning broadly. Baz and Ed force Bill to sit down on the sofa and pin his arms to his side. Jen and Angie take some of the records out of their cardboard sleeves and dash the discs against the walls, reducing them to jagged, black shards. Marky picks up several empty sleeves and laughs as he tears them into pieces.

The destructive trio ignore Bill's pleas for them to stop and turn their attention to the cassettes, whooping as they unspool the thin, brown tape. Finally, Jen grabs the red telephone and hurls it through the central glass panel of the bay window, accompanied by a loud scream of defiance. Marky stands directly in front of his pinioned victim, contemptuously kicking aside elements of Bill's life, shattered along with the memories held in each one.

'Sod the school project. This has been a right laugh! Besides, I reckon we've done you a favour, 'cos we're in 2039 not 1969, Grandad! Come on, you lot. We're off.'

Baz and Ed release Bill from their tight grip and join Marky, Jen and Angie as they head for the door. The five laugh and run down the steps into the street, leaving Bill's tears to fall amongst the vinyl splinters, tape ribbons and cardboard shreds.

HUMIDITY

A female figure stands motionless outside the house she shares with her husband (well, shares in the loosest sense). A bird sits completely still on a post to her right, and in front of the wooden building are two tubs of bright red flowers. The woman is wearing a long blue skirt, a white blouse and a red hat. She smiles as she looks straight ahead at the garden beyond and tries to ignore her husband's moaning.

'How long are you going to be out there, Heidi?'

'You know full well that I have no more control over that than you do when *you* emerge from your beloved shadows. Can't you leave me in peace, Hans?'

'Not really, wife, no, because life has bonded us to each other forever. I'm completely fine with that, but sometimes.... just sometimes....'

'Don't say it! Please don't say it!'

'What? I was only going to mention that sometimes I wish we could spend a little time together, that's all.'

'You can be so infuriating, Hans! You *know* that's impossible and, even if we could, we'd soon start arguing!'

'What makes you say such a hurtful thing, my love?'

'Because we're complete opposites, that's why! I *love* to look out from our little house on the mantelpiece. When the French windows are open, I can see the children in the garden, playing in the sunshine with their little kitten. You, on the other hand, or perhaps I should say the other *side*, only come out when it's drizzly, damp and dreary. I've never understood you, husband. Perhaps it's for the best that we don't share each other's company, after all.'

'Well, I can't help it if I prefer to stay here in the shade. You're welcome to the heat and, as for the sunshine, give me the sound of raindrops any day.'

'Typical! We're clearly as different as.... as different as.... oh, I don't know!'

'As different as sunny and rainy days?'

'Yes, that'll do, I suppose. Anyway, in answer to your initial question, it looks as if I'll be coming indoors later. There's a large bank of grey cloud moving in from the east, so your afternoon rest is going to be short-lived, husband.'

'Oh, well. Can't be helped, but at least you've had *some* time out there today. Our life isn't too bad, is it, Heidi? I know we only see each other in passing, but we'll always share this little house together.'

Heidi smiles to herself before responding.

'That *is* true, Hans. Despite our differences, we'll always have this little house.'

Unfortunately, that was not the case for much longer. Four days later, the kitten padded falteringly along the mantelpiece, wide-eyed with curiosity. It accidentally nudged the little house onto the wooden floor below, smashing the glass thermometer. The thin bar on which the couple had stood all their lives was also broken, so they lay together at last, side by side and gazing upwards. Their joy was brief, however, because within the hour they had been swept up along with the wreckage of their home, and unceremoniously tossed into the battered dustbin.

Such a shame, but then Fate, like the weather, can sometimes be rather.... mercurial.

A WINDOW TO THE HEART

Gary was always happy when he reached the last property on Castle Street. This was partly due to it being such a long road with a great many businesses to service, but mainly because the final shop was 'Bloomin' Perfect'.

He took a little extra time over the windows here, always happy when he caught a glimpse of Janice as she chatted to customers. Best of all was when she saw him through the glass and gave him a warm smile.

'Bloomin' Perfect' was quite a small shop, situated on the corner of Castle Street and Victoria Road, but what Janice lacked in space she made up for with colour. The interior was full of narrow, grey vases containing a wide assortment of seasonal blooms, from bright red tulips and orange dahlias to pink roses and white lilies. Janice had made excellent use of the property despite its limitations, even managing to include a surprisingly large table whilst not seeming to sacrifice retail space. She had also stacked upturned wooden crates towards the back, filling them with small pots of hyacinths and primulas in the spring, followed by marigolds and gazanias in the summer.

Gary had been a window cleaner for twelve years. He took pride in his work, successfully defending his patch from newcomers who often tried to muscle in. This was due to his hard-earned reputation for 'doing such a great job', a comment often voiced by his clientele. Lately, however, he'd noticed that his body was protesting more often, particularly his back, and it was becoming much harder to ignore. One of the few reasons for keeping going was his Friday round in Castle Street and the delight of seeing Janice again, albeit briefly. Also, the brightly coloured blooms inside the shop took Gary's mind off his back pain whenever he cleaned 'Bloomin' Perfect's windows, but it was only ever a temporary respite.

On recent Fridays, Janice had noticed Gary pausing more often as he worked outside, stretching his back and wearing a pained expression. She felt a wave of sympathy each time she witnessed his clear discomfort, but then chastised herself immediately afterwards. It was ridiculous, really. Janice only saw Gary on his weekly visits to her shop, during which hardly any conversation passed between them. Nevertheless, she always looked forward to the moments they were 'together' and felt a pang of emptiness each time she stood in the doorway, watching him walk away having been paid. She felt a need to alleviate Gary's physical distress, but how?

The idea came to Janice as she was opening the shop one Tuesday morning. Her first task that day was to complete a football-themed birthday tribute, due to be collected in the afternoon. Janice had designed the arrangement to look like a football, the main body comprising white flowers, with blue blooms used to form the pentagonal markings.

That was it! She would make something appropriate for *Gary,* something with a surprise inside that they might both enjoy. Perfect.

Janice had several large orders to fulfil that week, so knew that she wouldn't be able to work on Gary's present, even if she remained in the shop after closing time each evening. Besides, the surprise element required some consideration, so she planned to get everything ready in time for his round on Friday week.

~~~~

149

Janice watches as Gary puts down his squeegee for the third time. His back pain has clearly increased, and she can't bear to see him suffer anymore. She steps out of the shop with her arms folded and smiles.

'Could you just step inside for a moment, Gary? I've got something to show you.'
'Let me just finish off here first, Jan. I'll be with you in a minute.'

Nervous and excited about what she has 'in store' for him, Janice smiles and leaves Gary to complete his work. He enters the shop shortly afterwards, to find Janice standing near the worktable with a grin on her face. She lifts a large, lidded cardboard box and holds it out to him.

'This is for you, Gary, to thank you for all the times you've cleaned 'Bloomin' Perfect's windows. I hope you like it.'

Gary takes off the lid, reaches inside and lifts out a small window frame, expertly edged in white flowers. The glass has been removed and replaced with pale blue cellophane. He remains silent for a few moments, admiring the florist's artistry.

'It's lovely, Janice. I don't know what to say.'
'There's something else, Gary. Look inside the box again.'

Smiling broadly, Gary follows Janice's instruction and finds a white envelope, bearing the words 'A WINDOW BREAK'. Filled with curiosity, he opens it immediately and is astonished by its contents.

'Oh, Janice, thank you, but what made you think of going *there*?'

'I just thought a visit to The Shard seemed appropriate – thousands of panes of glass and you won't be able to clean any of them! I know it won't help with your back pain, but at least it will be a nice distraction for you.'

Gary looks at the ticket again and notices a further detail.

'This is for two people, Janice, so.... would *you* like to accompany me?'
'Oh, I'd love to, Gary!'

Janice's secret hope has come true and Gary, overwhelmed by her thoughtfulness, nervously gives her a hug.

~~~~

A romance will blossom as a direct result of that embrace and, over the next few months, Janice will persuade Gary to reduce his window cleaning workload.

They'll remember that first hug on their wedding day in just under two years' time, and everything will be.... 'Bloomin' Perfect'.

GRAPHOLOGY

It was laying on top of the other post when Freya got home from work, the envelope's turquoise shade contrasting sharply against the manila of those beneath. She picked the items off the mat, leaving all but the handwritten one on the kitchen table to open later and went through to the lounge.

Freya sat down and studied the envelope closely. She was intrigued, not only because she didn't recognise the handwriting, but also by the style and execution. The 'y' in Freya had a hard, right upstroke, and the flying bars on both 't's in Dutton were disconnected from the right side of their stems. The two words covered most of the surface, unlike the smaller, centred approach used by most people. She saw clear aggression in the writer's hand and felt uneasy as to what the envelope might contain.

As Freya ripped along the top edge, she wondered who might have delivered it. She had only lived in the flat for two months and had barely spoken to any of her neighbours. No-one engaged easily in conversation at work either, despite Freya's best efforts to engage with her colleagues. Her thoughts as to the author immediately disappeared, however, when she unfolded the single sheet of paper and read these words, written with somewhat more care:

PLEASE READ THIS LETTER CAREFULLY. WE WOULD NOT HAVE CONTACTED YOU ORDINARILY BUT, SINCE CERTAIN DETAILS HAVE BECOME KNOWN TO US, WE HAVE NO CHOICE.

FREYA, WE ARE WRITING TO YOU ABOUT YOUR NEXT BODILY INCARNATION. YOU WILL GROW UP TO BE KNOWN AS BRAD, A VIOLENT SERIAL KILLER LIVING IN SOUTH CAROLINA. YOU WILL MURDER TWENTY-FOUR PEOPLE OVER A PERIOD OF FIVE YEARS. YOU WILL HOLD EACH OF YOUR VICTIMS HOSTAGE IN YOUR BASEMENT AND SUBMIT THEM TO TORTURE FOR WEEKS BEFORE FINALLY KILLING THEM. DUE TO YOUR NOTORIETY, EMINENT PSYCHOLOGISTS WILL STUDY YOUR FORMATIVE YEARS AND CONCLUDE THAT THE SEEDS OF YOUR DEADLY RAMPAGE WERE SOWN DURING A TROUBLED CHILDHOOD.

THERE IS ONLY ONE WAY TO BREAK THIS CHAIN, FREYA, AND THAT IS FOR YOUR CURRENT LIFE TO END. WE KNOW THIS SOUNDS EXTREME, BUT WOULD YOU WANT TO INFLICT SUCH PAIN AND SUFFERING IN YOUR NEXT EXISTENCE, LEAVING SO MANY GRIEVING FAMILIES AND COMMMUNITIES RAVAGED BY FEAR?

Freya read the letter through several times, finding that final paragraph, and the question that closed it, deeply troubling. There was no name or signature on the letter, just a small arrow to indicate she should turn the paper over for more advice or information. What she read there shook her to the core:

YOUR DEATH IS ALREADY UNDERWAY, FREYA, BECAUSE YOU TRIGGERED A CHEMICAL REACTION AS SOON AS YOU TOUCHED THIS LETTER. JUST THINK! THIS SELFLESS ACT, ALTHOUGH NOT OF YOUR CHOOSING, WILL SAVE SO MANY FUTURE LIVES THAT WOULD OTHERWISE BE DESTROYED BY YOUR, OR RATHER BRAD'S, BLOODY HANDIWORK.

WE WOULD LIKE TO THANK YOU FOR YOUR CO-OPERATION IN THIS IMPORTANT MATTER AND APPRECIATE YOUR SACRIFICE, IN THE TRUE SPIRIT OF THE WORD.

GOODBYE, FREYA.

Freya panicked, screwed the letter into a ball and threw it across the carpet, as if this action might at least delay her demise. In amazement, she watched as the scrunched paper slowly rolled back towards her and unfurled itself at her feet.

A tingling sensation started to spread across Freya's body, as if small insects were crawling all over her. She rolled up her shirt sleeves, only to find that something far more unusual was happening.

Her full name, written in the envelope's angry hand, was repeatedly appearing across her pale skin. The words raised themselves in shiny, black welts and gradually merged, forming an excruciatingly painful mass. Consumed with agony, Freya tried to scream, but no sound emerged from her contorted mouth.

Before surrendering completely, she managed to look down at the letter which, as if waiting for her attention, set itself ablaze. Fire spread quickly through the apartment and, in amongst the crackles and spits, Freya heard laughter echoing through the smoke.

'NO 'TWO-LEGS' ALLOWED'

'Word' spread rapidly throughout both nests. Up in the apple tree, food-indicating pheromones were released in the intricate paper chambers and excitement grew. In narrow underground tunnels, antennae touched antennae which, in turn, touched more antennae, relaying the information seamlessly around the colony.

It was in the earthbound nest that those who had been above told those below what they had found. One of the 'two-legs' had discarded a square piece of chequered paper not far from the opening, so the initial foragers were soon joined by others to assist in the moving operation. Many pincers clamped along each edge of the napkin, and it was slowly manoeuvred into a shaded position under the apple tree.

The wasps didn't need to bring any food because, being late summer, there were several apples in various states of decay on the verdant grass. Some, however, found and killed smaller insects in the branches, dropping them onto the square as they flew down before landing. The ants had come across a dead mouse earlier that day, slowly rotting under a hedge near the tree. With some considerable effort, they managed to haul it onto the patterned paper, completing the preparations for this special occasion.

Hundreds of ants and dozens of wasps gathered during the late afternoon. Intelligent creatures all, with differing levels and types of memory, they had learnt to avoid places where groups of 'two-legs' feasted together. The wasps were always being swatted away, whereas the ants were often trampled on as they approached the spread of food. What did these massive creatures expect? Surely, they couldn't be surprised that, after laying out tempting, sugary delights, others would want to share in their abundance. No matter. There were no 'two-legs' around to disrupt *this* feast.

The 'event', however, didn't run smoothly, even without any human interference. The wasps gradually became intoxicated with fermented apple juice. They staggered around and crashed into each other on the square, vibrating their wings angrily whenever they fell over and tried to right themselves. A swarm of flies, attracted by the mouse carcass, descended on the proceedings. These gate crashers completely covered the small body, feeding frantically and denying the angry ants any access, even though *they* had done all the hard work.

~ ~ ~ ~

The following morning, a black plastic, two-talon claw descends on the napkin. Its operator grips the square tightly, shakes the dead mouse onto the grass, then releases the paper into his refuse sack. The 'two-legs' shuffles away from the apple tree, unaware that he has just left the scene of what could be described as recent waspish antics.

'Oh, well. We tried, but I can't say I'm sorry we couldn't help.'

'Me neither. I suppose we'd better get back to the palace, though, and *break* the news.... oops! See what I did there?'

'Careful.... you'll *crack* me up!'

'To be serious for a moment, I doubt very much if His Majesty will be that bothered. I reckon the only reason that he wanted *them* to assist was to cause more damage with their hooves, which they achieved when we rode back and forth over the bastard.'

'Where did he come from, anyway?'

'Dunno, mate. He just appeared one morning, sitting there wearing that smug grin and watching all the townsfolk going about their business. Did he ever make one of his oh-so-amusing comments to you, Jack?'

'No, thankfully, but my sister suffered his 'wit' last Thursday.'

'What happened?'

'She'd just been shopping at 'This Little Piggy'.'

'The new butcher's?'

'That's right, near the market. Anyway, Jill's usual walk to the shops takes her along the city wall, but she's chosen a longer route since *he's* been there. Her basket was rather heavy last week, so she decided to risk his 'merry mirth' and come back the old way.

She kept her head down and hurried past, but he must have seen her coming. Jill told me that he started chuckling and gurgling with delight, so proud of the terrible word play about to leave those thin, wide lips of his. Then, sure enough, out they came!'

'Go on, Jack, tell me what he said! I can take it.'

'Very well. Jill could only remember three of them, because she was trying to run away as he was still *punning* away. He said how '*eggs-ellent*' the weather had been lately and wondered what '*egg-citing*' things she had in her basket. Then, to top it all, he said that it looked heavy, but that the '*egg-cercise*' would do her good!'

'Dreadful! Did anyone ever find out what he wanted? Come to that, why did he choose *our* town? It was such a happy place before he showed up.'

'Exactly! Ironic really, because you'd think that a constantly smiling figure would add to our general sense of wellbeing, but no. His puns were so bad that....'

'Don't you mean *eggs-tremely* bad?'

'I'll ignore that! As I was saying, they were so bad that everyone started to resent him being here and wished him gone, or even dead.'

'I wouldn't be surprised if someone had pushed him rather than him just falling off. I mean, who could blame them?'

'I agree, and it could easily have been done under the cover of darkness. I heard that he didn't sleep and that his eyes used to twinkle in the moonlight, but it would only have involved creeping up from behind and giving him one hefty shove.'

'True, and his splattered remains *were* discovered at *crack* of dawn.'

'Stop it or I'll split my sides! But seriously, who found him?'

'Mr. Winkie. He'd just finished his usual night-time jog around the town and was on his way home. Wee Willie said it was a right mess and three foxes had already started feasting.'

'Well, there's nothing more we can do here. If we ride quickly, we'll get back before the palace kitchens close.'

'Great idea! What do you fancy for breakfast, Jack?'

'Only one choice, really. Scrambled eggs!'

TIME FOR NO CHANGE

A late evening in October. His least favourite time of year has come around again. The wrinkled, hunched figure sets down his hourglass, rests his scythe against the fireplace and sits down with a heavy sigh. A frown creases his deeply furrowed brow, and he grumbles his frustration.

'I mean, why can't everyone make their minds up? Some people like it when the clocks go back, whereas some of them hate it. Those northern dairy farmers are always happy with the extra hour of daylight because they don't have to work so long in darkness. Retailers, on the other clock hand, complain that far fewer customers shop after leaving work when it's dark in the evenings.'

He stares into the dancing flames and strokes his flowing white beard for a few moments, before his annoyance rises further.

'Oh yes, and then there are all those parents who complain that the darker mornings are more dangerous when their children are walking to school. Ridiculous, because most of their little darlings get ferried in cars almost to the school gates nowadays, so why are *they* whinging?'

He leans forwards to warm his bony fingers near the fire, then slumps back with renewed irritation.

'Also, what about all those polls and surveys that have taken place over the years? They haven't exactly helped, either. 52% in one say that people want to keep turning the clocks back and forth. Yet, in another, 84% say they want to have a constant measure of time. No conclusions, no agreement. On and on and on it goes. Well, I've had ENOUGH!'

The withered figure staggers to his feet, lifts his scythe as high as he can manage and crashes the blade down onto the hourglass. Shattered fragments and grains of sand litter the threadbare carpet, signalling the freezing of time forever. He closes his weary eyes tightly and mutters a spell to himself before opening them again, knowing full well the dramatic effects the incantation will have on the world. He grins, acknowledging the terror on the face of every static human, their eyes forced to remain permanently open to witness the unmoving scenes before them.

'That'll show 'em.'

The bitterness in his ancient heart remains intact, alleviated only slightly by a score having finally been settled. Now the only living figure able to move in his surroundings, the old man shuffles into the kitchen to make a cup of cocoa before going to bed. Half an hour later, he snuggles under his duvet with the clockface pattern cover, a sneer upon his heavily lined face.

'Goodnight, everyone, and sleep well! Oh, I was forgetting.... you can't now, can you?'

Old Father Time switches off the bedside light and starts to laugh.

'THE GREAT SURPRISO'

Vernon checks his props for the fifth time and his watch for the eighth. Tonight's performance is going to be the most important of his career. A live slot on national television! Who would have thought it?

When his agent rang two weeks ago to tell him about the booking, 'The Great Surpriso' was *so* surprised that he nearly fell over. The 1970s have been kind to acts such as his but now, as the decade draws to a close, stage magicians aren't regularly topping the bill anymore. Vernon noticed several empty seats during his last few shows, so he is only too aware that tastes are changing, which is why tonight almost feels like a revival.

Looking into the illuminated dressing room mirror, he appraises the large space, remembering all those tiny 'cupboards' in which he had to get changed when he started out on the club circuit. He faces his reflection with a broad grin and addresses himself.

'This room feels like a palace compared to them. Admit it, Vernon, you've bloody made it, my son!'
'Talking to yourself again, I see. That always used to drive me mad.'
'Sandra? But it can't be....'

Vernon's eyes search the mirror in vain, resting in defeat on his solitary image. Edged with contempt, the voice speaks again.

'Ah, but it *is*. Turn and face me, you rat!'

He spins around in his chair and is stunned into silence by the newly visible apparition. The upper half of Sandra's body hovers before him, whilst the lower moves independently, angrily pacing up and down.

Both are semi-transparent and appear to be illuminated from within. The disembodied images start to ripple slightly, which has an almost hypnotic effect on Vernon, until Sandra starts to shout at him.

'Allow me to remind you how it went. 'Oh, let me practice that well-loved trick,' you said! 'Just lie down here in this special box,' you said! I must have been *crazy* to trust you! I mean, I knew our marriage was in deep trouble, but not enough for you to do *that*!'

'I don't regret it for a moment, Sandra! You never believed I'd get anywhere with my act, and you were always putting me down. Well, look at me now, *darling* - 'The Great Surpriso' is about to hit the big time!'

A sharp knock on the door, accompanied by a young woman's voice, temporarily disrupts the argument.

'Are you alright, Vern? I could hear the shouting from *my* room. Who have you got in there?'

'Oh, no-one, Tara. I'm.... just trying out a voice I might use in the act sometime. Don't worry.'

'Well, we're first on tonight, so you've only got about fifteen minutes.'

'OK, I'll be with you shortly!'

'The Great Surpriso' and Sandra listen as Tara goes back to her dressing room. They glare at each other with utter contempt, but then the ghost's voice softens menacingly, unnerving Vernon.

'So, it's Tara now, is it? Pretty, is she? What a shame she'll be out of a job after tonight, but then you'll never work again, either.'

'You know what this evening means to me, Sandra. I demand you tell me why you're here!'

'Where's the fun in that? Besides, you'll find out soon enough.'

'Oh, just get back under the patio where you belong!'

'Charming! I thought you'd be pleased to see a *real* levitating woman for a change, rather than through your pathetic, so-called 'magic'!'

Sandra waves to Vernon as both parts of her body fuse together. She passes through the dressing room door, leaving him alone with his troubled thoughts.

~~~~

The red velvet curtains part with a soft swoosh. 'The Great Surpriso' and Tara walk hand in hand to the front of the stage, basking in the applause. They part with a flourish and the audience falls silent, ready to be amazed. The house lights are dimmed but, before the act can begin, Sandra appears in the wings and glides towards Vernon. She hovers directly in front of him then moves closer to whisper in rhyme, something *he* often does on stage.

'You tried to make me disappear,
Now say goodbye to your career!'

Vernon frantically looks at Tara, who gives him a confused shrug. Suddenly realising that only he can see Sandra, 'The Great Surpriso' feels distinctly uneasy. His dead wife glides towards the front row before addressing him again.

'Now, *darling*, I must go and find a good place to watch your little performance.'

Sandra waves and moves into the semi-darkness, whilst 'The Great Surpriso' desperately tries to concentrate.

The act opens with a retro classic. Sweating profusely and trembling with nerves, he starts to pull a string of coloured pennants from his right sleeve. Tara realises that something is terribly wrong, but she manages to maintain her fixed 'showbiz' smile. Just. She takes her end of the cord and slowly moves to the other side of the stage.

Sandra floats above the stalls and closes her eyes tightly. She focuses her revenge on the now fully extended row of brightly hued flags and the change begins.

The theatre and live TV audiences watch in amazement as letters form on the blue, green, yellow and orange triangles. Several are blank, but the message is still clear for all to see:

I K I L L E D M Y W I F E

The producer is heard to swear, the broadcast cuts early to an advertising break and disapproving murmurs ripple through the audience. Vernon and Tara look down at the altered prop and then at each other. Hesitantly, 'The Great Surpriso' tries to explain.

'Er.... I have no idea how this happened, ladies and gentlemen. Just some silly prank! Was it you, Tara?'

His assistant flashes him an icy look of contempt. No support there, then.

'What it says isn't true, everyone! My lovely Sandra left me last year and I was utterly heartbroken. Still.... best bloody vanishing act *I've* ever seen!'

No-one laughs or believes him, and the anger rises. Vernon feels the tide turning against him, but he struggles on regardless.

'How about some more magic? I've got plenty! Anyone? Please?'

Sandra splits in two, then positions her upper body near the circle balcony. She listens to the hateful shouts rising from the stalls, then laughs as several people storm the stage, shaking their fists and screaming threats. Tara runs to the wings in tears as punches start to rain down on 'The (now not so) Great Surpriso'.

Sandra's lower section wanders between the rows of seats, but eventually comes back to reconnect with her other half. She smiles as she wafts up the stairs to the doors marked 'EXIT', ignores them completely and drifts through the walls into the cold night air.

STINKY JACK

He appeared on the windowsill just as dusk was falling, and now looks out on the puddles growing ever larger on the patio, his grin widening as the family enters the kitchen. The sounds of complaint rise in the air and he listens to the voices growing louder, knowing his moment is fast approaching.

'But I want to go trick or treating, Mum!'

'I'm not letting you go out in this weather, Jamie, and that's an end to it!'

'All my friends will be doing it! They'll all laugh at me in school tomorrow and say I was scared to go out in the dark. It's so bloody unfair!'

'*Don't* swear at your mother, young man, and set an example to your little sister! Anyway, I agree with Mum. I've never been comfortable with this imported tradition, and I'm sure you've got some homework to do.'

Jamie kicks at one of the kitchen table legs in frustration, angry that Dad didn't take his side. He is about to run upstairs to sulk in his bedroom, when he notices that his little sister Rose is pointing up at the windowsill, her eyes gleaming with curiosity. Their parents have noticed as well.

'Who brought that thing in here? Did you spend all your pocket money on it just to spite us, Jamie?'

'No, I didn't, Mum! I'm glad it's there, though, because its broken one of your stupid rules!'

'Look, you *know* we don't approve of superstitious nonsense and want nothing to do with it in this house! Get rid of it, please, John.'

Jamie's father moves towards the window, but he stops when the thing slowly starts to turn. All stare into a pair of intensely yellow, glowing eyes. The uninvited guest's jagged grin widens further, as he surveys his victims and prepares to speak.

'Allow me to introduce myself. My name is Stinky Jack and I hail from Ireland. I lived a long time ago, but now I'm forced to roam the earth forever because of.... well.... let's just say a bargain that didn't quite work out for me. Even though I *almost* managed to deceive The Dark Lord and fully accept my punishment because of that failure, I am allowed the pleasure of tormenting anyone I choose on just one night each year. Unfortunately for you, this time round it's *your* turn to face me!'

Paula grabs her husband's hand, and they step forwards together to challenge the orange intruder.

'You are not welcome here, so go back to where you came from!'
'But my fun is just beginning! Why would I want to stop now?'
'You heard my wife! I insist that you....'
'Oh, do shut up! Here, let me help you with that.'

The yellow eyes suddenly burn even more fiercely, and John and Paula become aware of an odd tingling sensation about their lips. Stinky Jack laughs as the humans feel their mouths first diminish, then disappear completely. As they stare at each other in mute terror, Jamie and Rose start to cry, and their parents dread that their children will soon suffer the same fate. In sheer panic, John and Paula frantically hug their offspring. They face their tormentor, anger burning in their eyes, but Stinky Jack just offers a hollow stare in return.

'I knew you'd react like this. Every family I visit does, and you've already sealed your fate. Nothing can save you now!'

Consumed with fear, the group hold on to each other more tightly but, instead of experiencing familial comfort, find instead that their bodies are fusing together. Stinky Jack lets out a deranged laugh as his twisted creation, being made solely for his pleasure, takes shape.

Just before they become *completely* waxen, Stinky Jack uses his power to twist Paula's greying ponytail into a tight wick. He makes it stand upright, then aims a single stream of fire from his yellow mouth towards the top of what is now a human candle.

As the wick starts to burn and the wax begins to melt, Stinky Jack slowly turns to face the rain-spattered window once more, looking forward to *next* Halloween.

PAST PRESENTS

Molly lights another candle, wraps the pale blue shawl tightly around her and sits down in her mother's old rocking chair. She watches as the shadows dance on the walls and thinks back to last Christmas.

~ ~ ~ ~

Molly had been married to Bert for nearly fourteen years, in what she had always thought to be a happy union. The local gossip monger, however, had taken great pleasure in informing her that Bert had been seen canoodling with 'that little tart from The Bell Tavern' on several occasions. Bert came home drunk one night and Molly confronted him, at which point he smashed one of her few ornaments against the fireplace and staggered out into the December streets. She never saw him again.

~ ~ ~ ~

'Good riddance!' she says to herself as she now rocks back and forth to the gentle ticking of the clock on the mantelpiece. She glances up when the chimes ring for five o'clock, realising that the butcher's shop will be closing soon.

Molly steps into her well-worn shoes and hurries down the wooden stairs to her front door. The fog is so thick that it almost feels solid, having lingered since early morning. Molly doesn't think to wait before she crosses the cobbles, so is startled when a drayman's horse and cart loom out of the murk. She steps back and listens as the horse's hooves, along with the man's curses, fade into the dense greyness.

Even though Molly is on her own this yuletide and has tried hard to forget the first anniversary of Bert's hurried departure, she sees no reason not to indulge herself a little. Her usual shopping list consists of ordinary items such as bread, onions and potatoes, along with cheap cuts of meat for pies. She approaches the corner of the street with her heart (or, more accurately, her stomach) set on one of Mr. Green's succulent joints of beef. Molly does not earn much from her dressmaking job, but she has been saving what little she can for months, and now it all seems worthwhile.

~~~~

Molly needs to steady herself against the wall after turning into the main thoroughfare for fear of falling over. Whatever just happened? She had stepped out of the fog as if moving from one room to another and, although she can clearly see all that is spread before her, none of it makes any sense.

Molly sees a wide, smooth street ahead, with flat paved areas on either side. This is surprise enough for her, but the giddiness returns with a vengeance when she looks up into the clouds. There, clustered together, are vast towers of metal and glass, completely dominating the dark December sky. Molly stares open-mouthed at these edifices, until someone hurries past, knocking her shoulder in the process. Lowering her gaze, Molly stands in awe of the orange lights atop long metal poles. Such wonder! The gas lamps on *her* street provide only a dull glow through the fog but these, *these* are constant in their brightness.

Molly focuses her attention on the people around her, and she wonders why they are dressed so strangely. Most of the men look smart enough, although she wonders why none of them are wearing

172

hats, but several women are wearing trousers! One young slip of a thing has several rips in hers. They are made of a dark blue fabric, and Molly feels an urge to offer the girl her darning skills, but she decides against it. Besides, everyone appears to be in a hurry to be somewhere else, many of them carrying large bags filled to the brim with boxes and packages. Surely, they can't *all* be Christmas presents!

Molly thinks back to her childhood, when all she received each year was a wooden toy, handcrafted by her father. Not much, but it meant the world to her at the time and she kept all of them, now paint-chipped and scratched in the attic.

Perhaps the oddest thing Molly notices is how almost everyone appears to be talking to themselves, or rather, into something held near their faces. It seems to her that she can hear only one-way conversations as they hurry past. Hard as she tries, Molly just can't understand this, but then she sees something written on a board that *almost* makes sense to her.

The chalked message reads 'LARGE COFFEE £4.75'. Molly recognises the pound sign and, although confused by the numbers after the little dot thing, she understands the basic cost involved. Molly had tasted coffee before and wasn't too keen, but she can see that the coffee shop is fit to bursting with customers seemingly quite happy to pay. Bert had a steady job as a carpenter, but only got paid six shillings and sixpence a week, so how can people here afford *these* prices?

Molly decides to return home and away from this strange scene. It upsets her to find that all the shops she knew have been replaced by new buildings, and goodness knows where the bustling market has gone. She looks up at the huge gleaming structures again and fears that they might topple over at any moment, crushing everything in their path. This thought greatly disturbs her and she turns away, ready to flee, but movement to her right makes her stand stock still.

There are several curved, metal objects on solid wheels travelling at quite a pace on a much wider road between the buildings. How can they move without horses to pull them? Molly can see that there are people inside and she wonders if they are safe or somehow encased in moving prisons. Now scared as well as confused, she runs home as fast as she can.

~~~~

Molly steps onto the cobbles and the fog embraces her in its sulphurous grip, but she doesn't mind. Even the familiar stench of the sewers brings her reassurance that she is back home. She closes the front door and climbs the stairs, already planning to visit a different butcher for her Christmas meat in the morning. Happy that she won't have to enter that strange world again, Molly lights three candles and listens to a horse and cart passing near her window. The sounds of wooden wheels and hooves make her briefly close her eyes and smile.

Molly spends the evening making paper chains with which to decorate the main room and hallway. She enjoys cutting up old newspapers and even draws simple patterns on some of the links, but immediately feels the stab of loneliness in her heart as soon as the task is completed. Molly sits quietly for a few minutes and then, determined not to yield to melancholy, stands up purposefully. She utters a few curses aimed at Bert, then smiles at her little plan.

She clears the living room table of photographs and empty walnut shells, then fetches down her father's wooden toys from the attic. There are seven in all and she experiences intense pleasure at seeing them again. Placing the much-loved objects on the table, Molly feels happy childhood memories swirl around her, but then images from today crowd into her mind, cancelling out those innocent times. She closes her eyes in an attempt to shut out the intrusion, but it doesn't work.

~~~~

The massive buildings Molly saw in that other place now sway frighteningly in the vision, bending low and then rising again. Similarly, the bright orange lights on their grey poles follow her movements, as if studying her as she runs along the pavement. Molly sees the people in those strange, shiny carriages, pointing and laughing at her as they speed past.

Disturbed by their sneering faces, she trips and falls heavily onto the concrete. She attempts to stand, but someone pushes her down again. A crowd begins to gather and, as she looks up at the oddly dressed strangers, Molly starts to scream.

~~~~

Half an hour passes in the real world. Trembling violently, Molly slowly opens her eyes and looks around the candlelit room. The familiar surroundings bring her immediate comfort and her pained cries cease, although the shaking continues. In the stillness, Molly tries to understand today's experiences and the disturbing vision just encountered. Rather than making sense of either, only questions surface in her mind:

'*Why did I recognise the streets, yet know nothing about what I saw there?*
Was it a scene of what is to come?
Is this the beginning of madness?'

The internal queries repeat and tumble over each other, adding to Molly's unease. With no-one to turn to, she finds herself wishing that Bert were still around. At least, she thinks, he might hold her for a while which, in this moment, would mean so much to her. It is the painful memory of his cheating heart, however, that snaps her back into the present.

The shudders diminish as calm returns. Molly considers her humble circumstances and speaks out loud, with only the mantel clock to hear her:

'It's true Molly, my girl, you ain't got much and you're on your own but, if that place *is* the future, then you'd be better off living in the fog and stink right 'ere!'

With her body still shaking slightly, she pours a small glass of gin and raises it to the world outside.

THE THAW?

Everyone on Mistletoe Drive looks forward to the festive season. Wrapping presents, decorating the tree, all the usual fol-de-rol, except for two elderly sisters who have never seen eye to eye on anything.

Holly and Ivy Winters have lived next door to each other for nearly forty-one years. No. 24 was left to Holly in the family will, due to her being ten years older than her sister. Ivy, who never moved out of the area, jumped at the chance of buying No. 26 when it came up for sale, using most of her inheritance to purchase the small property.

They were so unalike in what they wore, their tastes in music and even their TV choices, but the starkest difference was between their temperaments.

From the day Ivy moved in, she would knock meekly at No. 24, or quietly call to Holly through the letterbox. Holly found this intensely irritating and would often pretend she was out when Ivy paid her a visit, grumbling to herself out of sight in the kitchen.

'Why did she have to move here, and why can't she leave me alone? The woman's so.... so.... clingy!'

Ivy's intentions were good, for all she wanted was some sisterly company. Neither woman had married, so Ivy assumed that Holly would be only too glad to have her younger sibling living next door. How wrong she was.

Ivy loved baking and excelled at it. Every few days she would tap on Holly's door and, when she received no answer, leave a floral tin containing her latest efforts before slowly walking back home. She knew what would happen. Within an hour, the tin would be returned to her own doorstep, the cake inside crushed by Holly's ungrateful fists. Nothing, however, seemed to deter Ivy's displays of kindness, and this drove Holly mad.

All Christmas ever did was intensify the chasm between them. From the start of each December onwards, Ivy would bring mince pies and stollen slices to No. 24 and, sure enough, they came back as shattered pastry, smeared mincemeat and icing sugar. Most hurtful of all was the fate of each Christmas cake, so lovingly decorated, yet hurled at Ivy's front door with real hatred. Last year, as Ivy swept up the splinters of white icing and splattered marzipan, she was sure that she heard Holly laughing from behind her snowflake-patterned net curtains.

The year before was even worse. Knowing Ivy's loathing for sprouts, Holly had posted the bitter little brassicas through her letterbox, one on each day of December, up to and including the big day itself. She had decorated them all with a grimacing face, inked on with a broad black marker. Ivy would have much preferred the present of an Advent calendar, rather than an Advent colander, full of the much-hated vegetables.

Ivy often sat and cried alone during the festive season, trying hard to understand her sister. What was the reason for such behaviour, and why did Holly prickle with so much hatred towards her?

Ivy had almost decided not to bother this year. She felt worn down by all that rejection and disappointment, but family traditions, however odd, are hard to ignore. So now, on the first day of December, she places a batch of still-warm sausage rolls, cushioned on red serviettes inside the floral tin, on Holly's doorstep.

Half an hour later, Ivy sits in her front room and waits for the usual response, but instead hears a gentle tap on the door. When she opens it there's no-one there, just the tin left on the front step with the lid askew. It is empty, apart from a few pastry crumbs and a handwritten note that reads:

THEY WERE DELICIOUS. THANK YOU.

Ivy, sensing that the ice might have started to melt in Holly's heart, rushes to No. 24 in her slippers and finds that the door has been left slightly ajar. She gingerly pushes it open and finds her sister in the hallway, smiling and holding out a glass of sweet sherry. Unable to hug (prickles don't fade *that* fast), Holly tentatively takes Ivy by the hand and they walk down the hall together.

Ivy goes to sit in the front room whilst Holly makes some tea. Although happy for the warm welcome, she is wary about such a sudden turnaround. After all the years of acrimony, can this *really* be happening?

Throughout the evening, Holly and Ivy reminisce about childhood Christmases, which proves to be a bad decision. Unspoken resentments on Holly's part rear their ugly heads, centred on her feeling that Ivy had always received better presents, and many more of them, because she was so much younger.

'You were *always* the favourite, Ivy, and I hated being in your shadow!'

'Oh, stop being so melodramatic, Holly! This is typical of you, playing the victim. Besides, you're wrong because we were loved equally. As for the presents, you should be grateful for what you *did* receive.'

'But you got *more*, Ivy! You know it's true!'

Clearly the ice is deeper and far more compacted than either sibling had realised, and the inevitable happens.

'Get out, Ivy! How stupid I was to think we could ever get along. Peace and goodwill? Stuff and nonsense, more like!'

'But I thought you'd started to change, and I was so happy.'

'Me? Why should I? Stay away from now on, little sister, not just for Christmas, but for ever!'

Muttering curses under her breath, Holly shoos Ivy out of the house and slams the front door.

Forlorn and disappointed, Ivy walks down the path, trying to come to terms with the painful truth that Holly will *never* change. Back in her kitchen, Ivy tears up Holly's 'thank you' note, then throws the pieces away. With a heavy heart, she opens the back door and tips the crumbs from the tin onto the patio.

Ivy looks down at the pale fragments on the paving. They somehow seem to represent the last vestige of hope, a hope cruelly snuffed out on this first day of December.

Oh, well. It will be a lonely Christmas at No. 26 after all.

'NEW YEAR, NEW ME - LIKE NEW'

She always loves New Year's Eve, but not for the reasons people usually give. Not for her the excuse to get pissed again so soon after Christmas Day, or those pathetic resolutions, most of which get broken by mid-January. No, her pleasure is much more specific and personal.

Each year, for the most part, she maintains a nutritious, nourishing diet, but November and December have always been a struggle for her. Over those two months, her energy levels sink dramatically, and she finds it hard to clamber out of bed each morning. Her skin looks like crumpled parchment, and what remains of her white hair sprouts in clumps on her pockmarked scalp.

Now, as so many times before, she sits on the bed and watches the hands of the bedside clock move towards her favourite hour. It is all beginning again, but she *must* concentrate.

10.40 p.m.

She listens to the revellers outside in the street, swelling both in number and noise levels. With considerable effort, she hauls her wizened body over to the window and draws back the curtain. Seven men are laughing and pointing at one of their friends, who has just fallen over on Edinburgh's famous cobbles. A group of young women walk past them, trying to ignore their raucous shouts and obscene gestures.

'They'll catch their death, those girls, dressed like that.'

She smiles at the comment and pulls the curtain closed. Pain and hunger take over as she sits on the bed again, but all she can do is wait.

11.15 p.m.

Too weak to take another look outside, she tries instead to focus her clouded eyes on the small clock. Frustrated by frailty, she listens to the rising whoops of laughter in the growing crowd and knows that there is not long to go now.

11.42 p.m.

Her hearing has started to desert her but, aware that this is the only sense she really needs at present, she strains to listen to what is happening. Some people are setting off fireworks early and, although for her the noise bursts are dulled, they add to her growing anticipation.

Midnight

Each strike of the clock further activates her renewal. Her wrinkled, useless skin falls away from her now perfect body and, on the strike of twelve, she stands and moves towards the window.

No longer wizened and feeble, she opens the curtain slightly. The fireworks bursting in the night sky reflect the fresh energy coursing through her naked frame, their colours dancing in her dark eyes.

Feeling an urgent need to get ready, she leaves the window, moves to her wardrobe and takes out a short black dress and matching shoes. It will be cold outside but, unlike those girls she saw earlier, it won't affect *her*. Sustenance awaits, warm, red and comforting on the streets of Edinburgh.

Having dressed, she returns to the window to listen to the happy throng, wondering who will provide her first and *very* special 'breakfast', so early on New Year's Day.

After locking up and skipping down the stairs, she pauses only to lick her lips before opening the front door. Stepping onto the noisy, vibrant street, she whispers to herself:

'New year, new me - like new.'